DELUDED

DI SARA RAMSEY #4

M A COMLEY

D1601184

JEAMEL PUBLISHING LIMITED

ACKNOWLEDGMENTS

Thank you as always to my rock, Jean, I'd be lost without you in my life.
Special thanks to Studioenp for creating such a superb cover.
My heartfelt thanks go to my wonderful editor Emmy Ellis @ Studioenp and to my fabulous proofreaders Joseph, Jacqueline, and Barbara for spotting all the lingering nits.

Thank you also to Claire Mawdesley from TBC for allowing me to use your name in this book.

And finally, thank you to all the members of my wonderful ARC group for coming on this special journey with me and helping me to grow as an author. Love you all.

DEDICATION

To Mary, I miss our chats when insomnia strikes. I hope you eventually found the peace you were searching for.

ALSO BY M A COMLEY

Immoral Justice (Book #17)

Toxic Justice (Book #18)

Overdue Justice (Book #19) Due out June 2019

Unfair Justice (a 10,000 word short story)

Irrational Justice (a 10,000 word short story)

Seeking Justice (a 15,000 word novella)

Clever Deception (co-written by Linda S Prather)

Tragic Deception (co-written by Linda S Prather)

Sinful Deception (co-written by Linda S Prather)

No Right To Kill (DI Sara Ramsey Book 1)

Killer Blow (DI Sara Ramsey Book 2)

The Dead Can't Speak (DI Sara Ramsey Book 3)

Deluded (DI Sara Ramsey Book 4)

Forever Watching You (DI Miranda Carr thriller)

Wrong Place (DI Sally Parker thriller #1)

No Hiding Place (DI Sally Parker thriller #2)

Cold Case (DI Sally Parker thriller#3)

Deadly Encounter (DI Sally Parker thriller #4)

Lost Innocence (DI Sally Parker thriller #5)

Web of Deceit (DI Sally Parker Novella with Tara Lyons)

The Missing Children (DI Kayli Bright #1)

Killer On The Run (DI Kayli Bright #2)

Hidden Agenda (DI Kayli Bright #3)

Murderous Betrayal (Kayli Bright #4)

Dying Breath (Kayli Bright #5)

The Hostage Takers (DI Kayli Bright Novella)

The Caller (co-written with Tara Lyons)

Evil In Disguise – a novel based on True events

Deadly Act (Hero series novella)

Torn Apart (Hero series #1)

End Result (Hero series #2)

In Plain Sight (Hero Series #3)

Double Jeopardy (Hero Series #4)

Sole Intention (Intention series #1)

Grave Intention (Intention series #2)

Devious Intention (Intention #3)

Merry Widow (A Lorne Simpkins short story)

It's A Dog's Life (A Lorne Simpkins short story)

A Time To Heal (A Sweet Romance)

A Time For Change (A Sweet Romance)

High Spirits

The Temptation series (Romantic Suspense/New Adult Novellas)

Past Temptation

Lost Temptation

Books to come.

Tempting Christa (co-written by Tracie Delaney coming in April 2019)

Avenging Christa (co-written by Tracie Delaney coming in May 2019)

The Man In The House (co-written by Emmy Ellis coming in May 2019)

PROLOGUE

TINA WEBB'S heart leapt with joy. It had been a while since she, Malcolm and the children had spent any real quality time together in the past few months, due to their obscene workload.

Malcolm had just started up a steam cleaning business, and she was helping him by answering the phone and being his general dogs-body, otherwise known as his secretary where his accountant and the taxman were concerned. It was tough embarking on the self-employed journey. Neither of them had gone down this route before; they'd always worked for large companies. Malcolm used to be a lorry driver, delivering goods for Marks and Spencer, and Tina used to work at a factory making Kipling cakes. She'd hated it, doing a mind-numbing job on the production line. She had endured the mundane role for years only because they needed the money. The upside was she got on so well with the rest of the staff. She missed them dearly.

But this was it now, the beginning of a new adventure for both of them—with the added bonus that she wouldn't have to rely on her mum any longer to care for the kids after school. Tallulah and Marcus were just as excited as her and Malcolm.

So here they were, up on the Brecon Beacons, Malcolm carrying the bulging picnic basket and the kids running around them, teasing Jasper, the black-and-white Cocker Spaniel.

"Happy?" Malcolm asked.

Tina pecked him on the lips. "Deliriously so. I don't think I've ever been so happy. Well, except when we walked down the aisle and the day I gave birth to the kids. Oh, and when I got that promotion at work."

Malcolm tipped his head back and laughed. "You're nuts."

"I know, but you still love me, right?"

He stopped beside her, placed the picnic basket on the ground and pulled her into his arms. "More than ever. I'd be lost without you in my life, Tina."

She kissed him again.

"Yuck, get a room, you two," Marcus shouted.

Tina turned to look at him and chuckled. His blond curls bounced in the breeze. She loved her family so much. Other mothers spent most of their time at the factory complaining about what their kids got up to. She'd never done that because in her eyes, Tallulah and Marcus were perfect in every way. They never fought, always played nicely together. Even settled down on the couch they snuggled up to each other, often with Jasper sitting close beside them.

Tina expelled a satisfied breath. "I'm so lucky to have you all in my life."

Malcolm slipped an arm around her shoulders and kissed the top of her head. "We're the lucky ones. Our business would still be a dream if you hadn't chucked your job in to help out. I know it's going to be a struggle for us over the next year or so, but I truly appreciate the sacrifices you've made."

"Nonsense. So, we forgo our holiday this year, and the money we've put aside for that will pay the bills until the business takes off. Do the kids look as though they're suffering? They're having a whale of a time, look at them. We're as solid as that boulder over there, we always will be. If the business fails, then we'll start over again. We've both got the right attitude to make this the success it needs to be. Now, less chat about the business, we're here to enjoy ourselves. How much farther do we have to go? My legs are killing me, and I'm starving."

Malcolm glanced behind him. They were approximately halfway up the large hill. He cringed. "We've got a long way to go yet before we reach the top."

She groaned. "I guess I'm not as young as I used to be."

He roared with laughter. "You're thirty-four, for God's sake. Old woman my arse," he said, lowering his voice so the kids didn't hear him swear.

"Okay, I'm not going to start an argument about this. I just want to enjoy our day out. Another few hundred feet up a steep climb isn't going to kill me, I suppose." She shuddered at the thought. She would need to dig deep to counteract the tiredness already seeping into her bones.

"Want me to give you a shove?"

"You might need to when we get near the top. Remind me, whose idea this was again?"

"You mentioned going for a walk. I picked the spot, though, as I recall."

"There's a walk and a bloomin' mountain climb. I think this can be deemed the latter. Me and my big mouth. I much prefer looking at the Brecons from a distance rather than climbing the damn things."

"Stop complaining. You're using up vital air. You'll need that when we get to the summit. The kids are fine, they're having a blast with Jasper."

She couldn't argue about that.

Half an hour later, they reached the summit. This hill was one of the smaller ones in the area, thank goodness. It was still a massive achievement to reach the top; they were all totally unfit. Well, she and Malcolm were anyway. The kids had oodles of energy and were still running around after Jasper.

Malcolm turned three hundred and sixty degrees, admiring the view, and pointed at the mountain in the distance. "It's still my ambition to climb that one day, Pen Y Fan. The tallest peak for miles."

"Make sure that's a day when you don't have me tagging along, okay?" Tina chortled.

THEY SPENT the next couple of hours sharing the sumptuous picnic Tina had spent the previous day preparing, which included sandwiches, a tuna and pasta salad and lots of different cakes, plus the odd piece of fruit thrown into the mix, too.

After eating, with her stomach bulging, Tina snoozed on the blanket for a few minutes before it was time to head back down to the car. One thing was for definite: they'd all sleep well tonight.

Once they were all piled in the car, they drove the hour or so back home.

Malcolm reached for her hand. "Thanks for today, the food was amazing."

"Wasn't it? You don't have to thank me, it's always a pleasure looking after my family."

They arrived home around four. The kids had the audacity to put in a request to stop off for a Big Mac on the way.

"Er, not likely, you two," Tina said, shaking her head when she turned in her seat to face them.

Marcus and Tallulah grinned.

"Ha ha, got you, Mum. We're stuffed. I don't think I'll be able to eat another thing all week," Tallulah said.

Tina laughed. "I'll hold you to that."

They unloaded the car and settled down to watch *Frozen*. It wasn't long before both kids were asleep in the chair. She and Malcolm carried them upstairs and put them to bed and then returned downstairs.

"Fancy a bottle of wine to finish off the perfect day?" Malcolm asked, hovering over her once she collapsed into the sofa again.

Her legs still felt a little wobbly from their adventure.

"Why not?"

They spent the next few hours with the TV switched off, chatting about the dreams they shared for the future and where they thought the business would lead them.

"By the end of the second year, I foresee us having twenty trucks on the go," Malcolm said enthusiastically.

"Really? That many, and so soon. I love your optimism. I hope you're right. Maybe we'll be able to buy that quaint little cottage out in the sticks we've always dreamt about owning."

"Who knows?"

The phone ringing interrupted their conversation.

Malcolm reached over and dislodged it from its docking station. "Hello?"

Tina tilted her head as he replaced the phone. "Who was it?"

"No idea. There was no one there."

"A wrong number then probably."

"I don't know about you but I'm ready for the land of nod. Gosh, never thought I'd hear myself saying that at nine o'clock. Let's finish off the bottle of wine in bed then, yes?" He stood and yanked her to her feet. "I love you, Mrs Webb. I still get shivers when I think of the time I almost lost you in that car accident a few years back." His eyes watered.

She ran a hand down his cheek. "You cared for me so well back then. I knew we'd be together forever, and that was before we were blessed with the children. Don't, I'm getting all emotional now. You know what I'm like when the tears start flowing."

He slipped his hand into hers and led her towards the stairs.

She planted her heels in the carpet to object. "Wait, I need to check the back door is shut, and Jasper will need a wee before we bed down for the night. You take the wine and glasses, I'll be up in a second."

He stomped up the stairs, never one for being quiet around the house—it was his only flaw. She let Jasper out and waited for her faithful companion to return. She topped up his water. He lapped half of it and then turned to walk through the house. He slept in their room on his own cot-sized mattress. He'd cried so hard when he was a pup being left alone downstairs that Tina had pleaded with Malcolm to bend the rules and allow him into the bedroom. That had been their undoing—he'd slept there ever since.

She locked the back door and switched off all the lights downstairs, her legs stiffening as she climbed the stairs. "Only a few more steps to go then you can rest for eight hours, I promise," she whispered.

She visited the bathroom, carried out her nightly routine and then slipped into the bedroom. Malcolm was propped up against the pillows, his Tom Clancy novel spread out across his bare hairy chest. She loved this man so much. Her heart still skipped several beats when she saw him half-naked.

Tina climbed into bed beside him and snuggled up. "Thank you for a lovely day. I feel so tired, I think I could sleep for a whole week."

"Go to sleep then. I just want to finish this exciting chapter and then I'll switch the light off."

Tina drifted off before he'd finished his sentence.

* * *

HE GLANCED up and saw the final light go out in the house. He'd leave it a while, it was still quite early to proceed with what he had in mind. He hunkered down in his seat, his balaclava in place already, surprised it wasn't irritating his cheeks. His gaze glued to the house in a trance-like state until he noticed the clock on the dashboard read five-thirty a.m. He finally left the vehicle, taking his equipment with him. He was relieved there were no streetlights in the immediate vicinity to highlight his movements. Sprinting down the alley beside the semi-detached house, he entered the back garden, ensuring he closed the gate properly. He crouched low and then ran across the lawn to the back of the house. He stayed there, perfectly still, listening for any movements in the surrounding gardens. When he thought the coast was clear, he opened his holdall and withdrew the small towel which he wrapped around his clenched fist. Within seconds he'd punched a hole in one of the panes in the back door. He inspected his hand in the moonlight—nothing, not even a slight graze. Replacing the towel in his bag, he slipped his hand through the hole he'd made, being extra careful not to cut himself on the remaining jagged glass still in position. He turned the key, opened the door and entered the house.

His heart pounded like an African drum, so much so that his breath hitched a little. He inhaled and exhaled several times to calm himself. Stood there a few seconds, listening. Once he thought the coast was clear, he continued on his journey through the house, each step taking him an eternity to complete in his efforts to remain quiet. He was aware the family had a dog and was determined not to alert it.

He placed his bag at the bottom of the stairs and withdrew another object, a can of petrol. He removed the lid inch by inch in his desire to keep the noise down. Then he went into the lounge—fortunately the door was still open, no chance of it squeaking when he entered the room. He poured some of the contents of the can over the sofa and the two armchairs and stepped back into the hallway. Then he tipped the can, aiming it at the front door, ensuring the family wouldn't be able to get out that way once the blaze took hold.

He rattled the can, judging there to be around a third of the petrol left, enough to do the bottom four or five stairs and the hallway going back through to the kitchen.

In the distance, a noise rumbled. Was that the dog growling? He'd need to be quick. Dousing the stairs and the hallway, he retreated into the kitchen and threw the remains of the can over the back door. He placed the can in the bag, then ran back through the house and extracted the matches he had in his pocket. He lit the first one in the lounge, the next one at the front door and the third one on the stairs as he retreated through to the kitchen where he lit the final match. The flames were already licking up the furniture. The orange glow lighting the house had a satisfying effect on him. He picked up his bag and darted across the lawn and out of the back gate. Making his way to the car, he glanced around him and grinned, nothing. He had got away with it, feeling no remorse or regret. Maybe that would sink in over the coming days, but he doubted it.

"That'll teach them. They shouldn't have done that to me... They're to blame, not me."

7

CHAPTER 1

THE WARMING SUN'S rays seeped through the gap in the curtain and lit up Mark's face on the pillow next to her. All was good in Sara's life. It had taken a while to finally get to this point, surmounting various challenges, but her ambition had now been achieved. She smiled down at him and then kissed him gently on the lips. "Good morning, sleepyhead."

He smiled, wrapped an arm around her waist and hugged her against him.

She wagged a finger. "As much as I'd like to stay here all day, I can't, I have work to do. Actually, so do you. Haven't you got a new assistant starting today?"

He scrubbed at his face. "So I have. Why do the weekends whizz past and yet the week always drags?"

Sara laughed. "Speak for yourself. Every day speeds past for me— too fast, in fact. I'll hop in the shower first. Oh no, you can get that twinkle out of your eye. That's a shower for one on the agenda." She kissed the tip of his nose and scooted out of the bed.

Misty, the cat, was lying on the quilt at the bottom, and she stretched. Sara ran her hand down the length of her cat's body. Misty purred, her excitement clear. *Yes, all is perfect in our world. The three of us have each other, and we couldn't be happier.*

Sara showered and cleaned her teeth then withdrew her navy skirt suit from the wardrobe and slipped into it, adding the red blouse Mark had bought her the week before. He was such a thoughtful man. Unlike any other she'd met—well, except for the first love of her life, Philip. Every now and then she mourned his loss, however, the pain of losing him was getting less and less with each passing day, now that she had Mark and they had declared their love to each other.

Mark swept past her and into the bathroom. She dried her hair and applied her makeup, then rushed down the stairs to see to Misty's needs. She was renewing the cat litter when Mark entered the kitchen, dressed in his jeans and a blue checked shirt.

"It's all very well buying me a new blouse; when was the last time you spent any money on your own wardrobe?"

"You're worth spoiling. I have enough clothes. What you're really saying is that you're bored with me wearing the same clothes all the time. I admit, it does get slightly monotonous. I forget and just grab the first thing I lay my hands on. It's a good job I wear a uniform eh?"

"I should say. Your customers might be concerned otherwise. Did you say you'll probably be late tonight?"

"Yes, I've got a tricky operation to do on a Doberman around six to try and fix his broken leg. It's going to be touch and go if I'll be able to save it or not. *Supervet* I ain't. That miracle worker is giving us mere mortal vets a bad name. People watching his show think all vets can perform miracles like he can. Anyway, don't get me started on that. I should be home about nine. I'll let you know. How do you think your working day will pan out?"

"My desk is relatively clear at the moment." She clicked her thumb and finger together. "But it can change just like that. We've had our share of tough cases to contend with as a team, we deserve a breather for a week or two."

"Famous last words. You've probably tempted fate now. Want a piece of toast or do you have to shoot off?"

"You see to the toast, and I'll make the coffee. I've got ten minutes before I have to leave. If I delay it any longer, I'm going to hit the traffic on the edge of town. I envy you having your surgery just up the road. You never get delayed on your way into work, do you?"

"Nope." He tapped his forehead. "That was intentional. When I was on the lookout for a surgery, I ensured it was on the outskirts of town. It seems to have worked out for the best, too. Hardly any of my clients miss an appointment or show up late."

"Clever dick. Unfortunately, the nick is in the heart of the city. I swear the traffic gets worse every damn day." She poured the boiling water over the coffee granules and sugar and added a splash of milk to the mugs just as the toast popped up for Mark to deal with.

"Butter or marmalade on yours?"

"I fancy butter this morning. I'll ring Mum tonight, invite us over there for Sunday roast. Are you up for that?" She saw Mark hesitate while buttering the toast. Placing a hand on his back, she asked, "What's wrong? Is it too soon?"

"Let me think about it and get back to you tonight. Maybe it is too soon. I love spending time with you, being alone with you in the house, it's a safe environment."

A smile touched her lips. "I get where you're coming from. They'll be gentle with you. You won't meet a more understanding couple, I promise you."

"Not that you're biased or anything." He laughed and carried the plates over to the small kitchen table.

"I suppose you're right. I'm guilty of wanting the world to know we're serious about each other. There's no better place to start than with our parents."

He blew out a breath. "I know I don't talk about my parents much. It's not that I don't love them, I'm just not sure I'm ready to introduce you to them—purely selfish reasons on my part. He covered her hand with his.

"I accept that. Whenever you're ready to make the leap is fine by me. The next time I see Philip's family I'm going to tell them about you. I've held off doing that up until now, not knowing how they'd take the news, but now, I want the bloody world to know we're together and in love."

"There's no rush. I'll leave that side of things up to you. I'd prefer to leave my folks out of it for the time being. It's not as if we're in each other's pockets all the time. They're busy people and tend not to pester me, which suits me."

She coughed to clear her throat. "Do they even know about me?"

He hung his head in shame. "Believe it or not, I'm a totally private person, or should I say, I used to be. So much has changed since I met you. Maybe...you know, me being abducted has changed my outlook on life. I don't know. Anyway, I'm happy to keep Mum and Dad at arm's length and things just the way they are. Let's just say they take a little getting used to."

"Now all that's done is alert my intrigue gene." She finished off the last mouthful of toast and stood. "I've gotta fly. Will you lock up for me?"

"Of course. You go. I'll see you later."

They shared another kiss. Sara grabbed her keys off the table and rushed into the hall to put on her shoes and coat, although she debated wearing the latter with the sun shining so brightly. She'd take it just in case, knowing how changeable the British weather could be.

Sara arrived at the station just shy of twenty minutes later. She spotted her partner's car already in the car park, nothing new there. "Morning, Jeff, all quiet overnight?" she asked the desk sergeant as she walked through the reception area.

"There's a note on your desk." He raised his hand. "That's all I'm prepared to say, ma'am."

Studying him closely, Sara noticed there were tears in his eyes. She didn't push the matter; instead, she ran up the stairs two at a time and swept through the incident room into her office. She plucked the note from her desk and read it. A lump formed in her throat, and her own eyes misted up. She dropped her bag on the floor and returned to the incident room to address the team. "Morning all. Not sure how aware you are of this." She waved the note. "Looks like we have an arson attack on our hands. Carla, are you ready to rock and roll? We should get over there ASAP." Carla nodded but remained silent. "I don't have to tell you guys what to do. Let's get the usual checks done on the property and its inhabitants. We'll be back soon to fill you all in."

Sara nipped into her office and picked up her handbag.

Carla was waiting for her at the door, her head bowed, showing how upset she was at the thought of attending the scene.

They left the room.

Sara touched her partner's arm at the top of the stairs. "Are you all right?"

"I'm fine. Hate to be involved in such tragedies. Why wipe out a whole family like that?"

"That's what we've got to find out. Chin up, sweetheart."

Carla walked down the stairs ahead of her, her shoulders slouched.

Sara sighed. She wasn't looking forward to dealing with the case either, but she knew they had to put their own feelings aside for now and do the family justice.

In the car, searching for a distraction after she'd keyed the details into the satnav, she asked Carla, "I'm dying to hear how your date went on Saturday?"

Carla turned her way and raised an eyebrow. "Do you think that's appropriate at a time like this?"

Oh, okay, slap me down for being an insensitive bitch, why don't you?

"Sorry. I'll concentrate on my driving instead."

"You do that," Carla snapped, unnecessarily.

Sara wondered what was eating her partner, whether the case had already got under her skin or whether her date on Saturday had been a total disaster and Carla was keen to avoid the topic. She'd keep her mouth shut instead during the ten-minute journey.

The plumes of smoke could still be seen and appeared to be drawing them to the location.

"Crikey, this is a bad one."

Carla's head swivelled slowly to face her. "Really? Is that the best you can say?"

"Whoa, don't take your foul mood out on me, missy."

"I'm not. Just stating that you tend to come out with the obvious at times. That ticks me off."

Sara drew the car to a halt alongside the first fire engine. "You need to rein in that temper of yours, Carla. I'm not about to take any shit from you over this, got that?"

Carla heaved out a large breath and voiced a quiet apology. "Sorry."

"What's going on?"

Carla tightened her hands into fists and repeatedly released and clenched them a number of times before she replied, "Nothing. All's good with me and my perfect world."

"So your foul mood is personal then, nothing to do with the fact that a family has been wiped out in this tragic event."

"Your words, not mine. It has everything to do with this event."

"What? You're not making any sense. Spill?"

Carla reached for the handle and tried to get out of the car, but she'd forgotten to unclip her seat belt. "Damn." She banged against the headrest, defeated.

"What the fuck is your problem?"

"Nothing. Don't do this, boss. I'm fine. I'm dealing with it in my own way."

"Dealing with what? Jesus, tell me?"

"My date on Saturday was going really well until…"

She gasped. "No, he didn't try anything on. Did he lay a hand on you? We'll get him if he did, I promise you."

"Will you listen for a change instead of jumping to conclusions? No, he was the perfect gentleman." Carla stared off into the distance.

Sara's gaze followed hers. She was transfixed by the firemen tackling the blaze. "Then what?"

"He's one of them."

"No! He's gay?" she asked, gobsmacked.

Carla faced her and shook her head. "Not one of them, one of *them*." She pointed at the men holding the hoses.

"Wow, he's a fireman. Sorry, I'm not with you. I don't see what the problem is."

14

"It's a dangerous job. What if I fall for him and he ends up getting killed while he's trying to put out a fire?"

"Hello, news alert! You're a copper, that's an occupation that is ranked highly dangerous on the scale of jobs to avoid doing if you're of a nervous disposition, too, in case you hadn't noticed."

"Bugger, I know that. Shit, I knew I should have kept my mouth shut. Now you're going to think badly of me."

"You talk a bucketload of crap at times, lady."

"Do I?"

"Of course you do. You're looking for excuses not to enjoy life. Look, as much as I'd love to continue this conversation, now is not the time."

"Sorry, you're right. I'm being a selfish cow, as usual."

Sara left the vehicle and slammed the car door. "You're not. So stop thinking that way."

Carla joined her. They had their IDs in their hands and showed them to the uniformed officer manning the cordon. He held the blue-and-white tape up so they could duck under it. There was a SOCO team on site, and Sara spotted Lorraine, the pathologist, leaving her van. She headed that way to speak to her, noting that the fire appeared to be in its final stages now, thanks to the sterling work of the firemen on duty.

"Lorraine. Too early to tell us what you know, obviously."

"Yep. Not sure why I'm here really. There's no way our guys will be able to get in there for at least a day or so. That'll be after the fire investigation team have done their bit. Shocking, all the same."

"I know. Do we know anything about the family? Did anyone manage to get out?"

"Mother, father, and two kids aged five and seven. No humans made it out, but the dog over there was flung out the window by the father, so the neighbour said." She pointed at a woman holding a leash with a Cocker Spaniel on the end.

"How strange. Maybe the dog was in the bedroom with the husband and wife, and they both went back into the house to rescue the kids and got trapped."

"Possibly. My guess is when the husband opened the window, it fanned the flames and made the fire worse."

"How terrible. Is the woman the neighbour?"

"The neighbour is the woman on the right. The one on the left is the mother of the woman who perished in the fire."

"Shit! Who called her?" Sara asked, staring at the distraught woman.

"The neighbour. She got out as soon as she heard the screams going on next door and called nine-nine-nine immediately. Her home has been affected by this, too. Sod's law when you own a semi-detached, I suppose."

"Bugger. Okay, I'm going to have a word with the man in charge, see what he can tell me."

"Let me know what he says."

Sara and Carla approached a fireman who appeared to be dishing out the orders. Sara flashed her ID. "DI Sara Ramsey, SIO on the case. This is my partner, DS Carla Jameson. Can you give us a clue what's going on?"

"Mike Green, senior officer in charge. We've been tackling the blaze since around six this morning. It's died down a couple of times but started up again. One of my lads got in there. I wouldn't allow him to go too far, though. From the smell he could tell an accelerant had been used."

"Accelerant, such as?"

"Smelt like petrol. That's when I decided to call you lot in."

"Thanks for that. There was no chance of getting in there to try and save the family then? I'm not judging you, just asking the question."

"It was raging out of control when we got here, too dangerous for my men to go in there when an accelerant has been detected."

"I get that. The poor family. Anything else you can tell me?"

"Nope. Only the basics until the fire investigator has been over the place."

"Thanks. I'd better have a word with the neighbour and the mother then."

"You do that," he said, paying attention to the younger man who had approached him.

Sara glanced at Carla and noticed her cheeks were as hot as the fire thirty feet away from them. She nudged her in the ribs and together they walked towards the two women she wanted to interview. "Was that him?"

Carla nodded. "Yes."

"Bloody hell. He's *gawjus*. You need your head read, my girl, if you consider dumping him. That's all I'm going to say on the matter."

Carla laughed. "Okay, I'll book an appointment with a shrink next week, how's that?"

"Do what you like. That'll be a hundred quid wasted."

The two women were leaning against the wall of a neighbouring property, staring at the house. They both appeared to be in shock.

"Hi, I'm DI Sara Ramsey, and this is DS Carla Jameson."

The woman wearing a pink velour dressing gown with rollers in her hair smiled briefly. "I'm Sylvia Trent, I live next door. My house has been affected, too, but that doesn't matter. This is Tina's mother, Cynthia. We believe Tina is still in there…" Her voice trailed off, and she pointed a shaking finger at the burning house.

"I'm sorry. It's a tragedy this has happened. I appreciate how upsetting this must be for you both. We need to ask a few questions, if that's all right?"

Both women nodded.

"Sylvia, we suspect the fire was deliberately started. Did you happen to see anyone suspicious hanging around the house before the fire began?"

"No. I'd been in bed for hours. The shouting around five-forty woke me." She gulped, and tears flowed down her cheeks. "I'll never forget their screams as long as I live."

"I'm sorry you had to hear that. You rang Cynthia, yes?"

"I rang nine-nine-nine and then called Cynthia straight after. I knew she'd want to be here. That's right, love, isn't it?" She patted Cynthia's hand.

The poor woman seemed lost, her gaze flitting between Sara,

Carla and Sylvia then back to the house. "Yes. My poor babies, what am I going to do without them? They were my life."

"Is there anyone else we can call to be with you, Cynthia?" Sara asked, a lump bulging in her throat.

"They were the only family I had left. I lost my mother and father last year, and now...they've all been taken from me." She broke down and sobbed.

Sylvia cuddled her. "There, there. The police officers will find the culprits, love. Won't you?" she asked, glancing over Cynthia's shoulder.

"We're going to do our best. Did either your daughter or your son-in-law mention if they were having problems with anyone?"

Cynthia leaned back against the wall. "No. Nothing like that at all. They got on with everyone. They were helpful, loved their family. Always put the kids first. They'd just started up a new business. Maybe...that will help."

Carla jotted down some notes without Sara needing to ask her to. "Perhaps. What type of business?"

"Steam cleaning. They had big plans, were going to grow the business quickly to employ more people."

"How long has the business been up and running?"

"A week or two."

"I see. And what did your daughter and son-in-law do for a living before that?"

"Tina worked on a production line at the local cake factory, and Malcolm was a lorry driver. He was away from home a lot. That's why they saved up enough money to become self-employed. He felt he was missing out on seeing his family grow up...and now this..." She shook her head, her eyes wide with disbelief.

"Poor Jasper, he was the only one to get out. They loved him; he was a treasured part of the family," Sylvia said. "Malcolm must have thrown him out. He landed on the hedge. I rescued him and ran into the house to fetch one of my old leashes for him."

Sara looked down at the dog which was sitting, staring at the blaze. "Where will you stay, Sylvia? You will probably be unable to access your house for a few days."

"She can come and stay with me," Cynthia replied. "Jasper can come, too. I won't see either of them out on the street."

"Did your daughter mention if she'd seen anyone lurking around the house lately? Someone possibly following her, anything like that?"

"No, nothing. I can't believe anyone would go out of their way to deliberately hurt any of them."

"Okay, we'll leave it there. I'll give you both a card. Ring me if anything comes to mind."

"We will," Sylvia said, taking both cards and thrusting them into her dressing gown pocket.

"Can you give Carla your address? We'll check in with you in a few days."

Sara walked away from the group of people and turned to look at the fire, then her gaze fell onto the bystanders—all neighbours? Or were they? Was the arsonist standing amongst them? Admiring his work in a sadistic fashion? She'd organise house-to-house enquiries, see if anyone had seen anything out of the ordinary. The family seemed to be as normal as they come. Why would anyone want to hurt them? She made her way back to Lorraine to fill her in.

"Anything useful?" Lorraine asked, running a hand through her shocking red hair.

"Nothing. A run-of-the-mill family, wiped out for no apparent reason."

"Heartbreaking. Secrets?"

"Possibly. Either that or mistaken identity?"

"No way." Lorraine shuddered. "That caused a chill to run through me then."

"Not unheard of, you know that." Sara glanced back at the two women. "Bloody hell, they're both going to live with the nightmares of knowing the family screamed before they died. I often think victims lost in a fire die of smoke inhalation. Apparently, that was far from the truth in this case."

Lorraine shuddered again. "Doesn't bear thinking about. Those poor kids. Just starting out in life and to have it snuffed out in this way. Crap, I hate this world and the bastards who inhabit it at times. I could go into detail about what the body goes through when consumed by smoke and fire—it ain't pretty. No one deserves to go out like that. No one."

"I can imagine. I don't want to know the ins and outs, I'm upset enough about this as it is."

Carla joined them a few seconds later once the conversation had stopped and their gazes were transfixed by the fire. "When you walked away, Sylvia said she remembered pulling her curtains around eleven before she got into bed and thought she saw a man sitting in a dark car."

"Excellent. Does that mean the man watched the house all night before he lit the match?"

Carla shrugged. "Pass. I wouldn't get too excited. She couldn't tell me the make or model or even give me a partial number plate. So we're no further forward."

Sara closed her eyes for a moment. "Damn." She opened them again and shrugged. "That leaves us up shit creek. There are no CCTV cameras around here to help us."

"Want me to arrange the house-to-house enquiries? If Sylvia saw the car, the odds are in our favour that one of the other neighbours possibly saw it, too, and they might be able to give us more details."

"Okay, do that for me, Carla. The sooner we get that information the better."

Carla held up a finger. "One more thing. Sylvia also mentioned that Tina was part of the Neighbourhood Watch team. She also cared for a couple of the more elderly residents in her spare time during the day. Unpaid caring. It was the type of person she was. Gentle, kind and considerate, plus the kids were absolute angels, apparently. No bother at all."

Sara tutted. "Well, that just sucks and makes this case even more harrowing than we first thought. Nice, well-loved families rarely get killed off. So either someone was hiding a secret or..."

"Or?" Lorraine prompted, frowning.

"We've got a possible pyromaniac on the loose. They don't need an excuse to start a fire, do they? Heck, listen to me. I'm probably talking out of my arse."

Carla shrugged. "Nope, you could be onto something."

"I agree," Lorraine added.

"I hope not. We had a case like that up in Liverpool, only the perpetrator purposely targeted businesses and not private residences that were occupied. Only two people died. I say only, you know what I mean. We've had four here tonight. God, I hate this frigging job sometimes."

Lorraine dug her in the ribs. "No, you don't. Because you'll bust a gut to ensure you get this fecker off the streets ASAP. That's what keeps the spark alive. Yes, you have to deal with the shit of consoling the victims' families in cases like this, but that also gives you the determination to bring the bastard to justice. There, I've done my part. Feel free to add anything, Carla."

"I think you summed it up perfectly," Carla replied.

Sara nodded. "Okay, you guys win. Maybe I don't hate the job as much as I thought I did. Come on, Carla. We have things to organise."

CHAPTER 2

HE SAT in his crummy bedsit, staring at the TV. He'd been like that all night, hadn't slept a wink since he'd got home around six a.m. ITV News had a yellow strip running across the bottom of the screen: **ARSON ATTACK IN HEREFORD. FAMILY PERISHES IN THE FIRE.**

Numbness consumed him. No feelings of remorse at all, not like he'd expected. He could get used to this. Robbing folks of their lives. The fire was dying down now, he could see that over the reporter's shoulder. She was trying to get a response from the detective in charge at the scene.

"DI Ramsey, a quick word if you will. I'm Carol Whittaker from ITV News. Can you tell us how the fire was started?"

The detective was attractive, blonde, slim build, thinner than he usually liked his women, but he suddenly felt attracted to her for some strange reason. Morbid fascination, perhaps because she was going to be the one tracking him down? He focused on her vivid blue eyes, the reflection of the fire burning within them. His erection grew. It had been a while since a woman had affected him in such a way. In all honesty, he thought such feelings had died long ago.

Wow, what a beauty!

I bet you'd like a piece of her arse.

The voices started up inside his head.

This woman had something special about her. She came across as hard but caring. Saying all the right things about the Webb family and promising to hunt down the person responsible for starting the fire.

"Petrol, you say. Do you have a suspect in mind?" the reporter asked.

The detective nodded. "At this point we have several leads to follow up. That's not to say we wouldn't be interested to hear what other residents have to say. We're carrying out house-to-house enquiries in the neighbourhood now."

His eyes narrowed. "Several leads, eh? That's a load of bullshit! Maybe I got you all wrong, Inspector Ramsey. There was me thinking you were different from the rest. You're not!"

"Well, thank you for speaking with me, Inspector. Good luck with your investigation."

"Thanks." The detective walked away, back to a group of people standing by a van.

"Back to you from this tragic scene, Jemma." The reporter handed back to the anchor woman who dismissed the story as if it meant nothing.

That's the world we live in. The living suffer every day of their working lives in one form or another, and the dead are discounted as soon as their deaths emerge. What a world!

He picked up his notebook and wrote down the detective's name inside the front cover, in a prominent position where it wouldn't go unnoticed every time he opened the book. Then he studied what was next on his agenda. The list of names was extensive. Running his finger up and down, he chose his next victims. He'd spend the next few hours confirming everything was in place. Then he'd get out there, follow them, ensure all of them were at home when he struck. He hated having any loose ends to tie up. He grinned, threw the book aside on his bed and switched off the TV. He was tired now, dead tired. His eyes drooped, shutting out the images of his devastation, the first of many to hit this town. He stirred and picked up his notebook again to jot something down: *return to finish off the neighbour, when time permits.*

He fell asleep within moments, his dreams filled with excitement at what lay ahead.

CHAPTER 3

THE TWO DETECTIVES returned to the station. The journey was silent, both of them wrapped up in their own thoughts. Sara even forgot to rib Carla about her new fella en route.

Sara trudged up the stairs on heavy legs. What she hated most about the case was the fact there were kids involved. She didn't have a maternal bone in her body, not that she knew of anyway, but that didn't mean she didn't care when she heard about kids losing their lives.

Barry sought her out as soon as she entered her office to immerse herself in dreaded paperwork after she'd instructed the team on what needed to be done. "Ma'am, the chief rang while you were out. Told me to ask you to ring her ASAP."

"Thanks, Barry. Be a love and get me a coffee, will you? I get the impression I'm going to need one."

Barry left the office.

She picked up her phone and dialled the chief's direct line. "It's DI Ramsey, ma'am. You wanted me?"

"Ah yes, nothing important. Just ringing up to see how things are. Personally, I mean."

"Oh right. Yes, everything seems to be back on course. Mark still has times when he glazes over, obviously reliving his ordeal, but they're becoming less and less now."

"Good, good. Time is a great healer. Are you dealing with the arson case?"

"That's right. Not much to go on yet. Nice family, apparently. No enemies that the mother can think about just yet. She's in shock, so who knows what she'll come up with when she's had time to think things over?"

"Give her space. Terrible tragedy to contend with. I saw it on the news a few minutes ago. You look good on camera."

"Thanks. I felt like shit talking to the reporter. Beefed it up a bit, told her we had several leads just in case the killer was eagerly watching the news report. I wish that was the case. The neighbour saw a man sitting in his vehicle, but that's as much as she could tell us."

"Damn, not good. I take it you're carrying out house-to-house enquiries?"

"Yep, uniform are on it now. I'm hoping that will give us something to work with. We've got very little else to go on at this point. Background checks on the family are being carried out by my team. Hopefully we'll have something that sparks an interest soon. Until then, I'll have my head down in the usual crappy paperwork."

"You and me both. Okay, I'll let you get on. Keep me informed."

"Will do." She ended the call the same time as Barry deposited her cup on the desk. "Anything yet?" She waved her hand. "Don't answer that. I know it's far too soon."

"Nothing yet, boss. I'll get back to it."

Sara left her chair and glanced out of the window at the view of the Brecon Beacons beyond, hoping for inspiration, but nothing came. She returned to her desk and rang her mother while she drank her coffee. "Hi, Mum. How are things?"

"My, what a pleasant surprise. We're fine, darling. How's work?"

"Not bad. Any chance I can come over for Sunday lunch this week and bring a possible plus-one?"

"Of course. Is this that young man you've been dating and keeping from us?"

"No flies on you, Mum. It wasn't intentional, I just needed to see how things worked out for us before I introduced him to the family." She'd kept the trauma that had touched hers and Mark's lives over the past few months from her parents, not wishing to worry them, especially as her father was under a specialist for his ticker.

"That's understandable. Philip is a tough act to follow. I hope your heart has healed enough to cope with a new relationship, Sara."

"Don't worry, Mum, I'm pretty confident it has. You're going to love Mark, he's the local vet. I met him when… Umm, I took Misty for her yearly vaccination," she added quickly, avoiding telling her mother that her beloved cat had been poisoned and almost lost her life in the process a few months before, at the beginning of their troubles with the gang connected to her husband's death.

"How wonderful to have a vet in the family."

"We're dating, Mum, nothing more yet. Don't go getting ahead of yourself now. I'm an independent woman. It's going to be hard relinquishing the freedom I've grown accustomed to since Philip's death."

"I know, dear. But it'll be nice to have a bit of company for you. We worry about you being in that house all alone. I know I haven't said it before. There, I've said it now."

"You're daft. I'm fine. A savvy policewoman, don't forget."

"Who has a vulnerable side. The people you work with might class you as an ogre, but I know differently."

Sara tilted her head back and laughed. "I am not an ogre at work. My team are the best around for a reason, because we all get on and work well together. They really are a blessing in disguise at times. I only have one who shows his eagerness too often; Craig is getting there, though. He'll make a great copper in the not-too-distant future. Anyway, I didn't ring up to discuss work. Can we bring anything on Sunday? Oh, and can we ease Mark into things first? Which means don't invite the tribe over."

"Oops, lucky you said. I was in the process of planning a big family lunch which included Timothy and Lesley. I do wish you guys found more time to see each other."

"I regret not getting in touch with my brother and sister more than I do. It's called life getting in the way, Mum. Hopefully things will settle down enough in the near future. Have either of them said anything?"

"Of course they haven't. I notice things, that's all. Still, it'll soon be summer. We'll get everyone together for a large barbeque, how's that?"

"Sounds ideal. Thanks, Mum. See you around twelve on Sunday. Give Dad a hug from me."

"I'll be sure to do that. Have a good week. Love you."

"You, too, Mum." She hung up and sipped at her coffee then buried herself in her paperwork for the next hour.

The stirring of a headache came on, so Sara popped a couple of paracetamol and washed them down with the remains of her coffee, shuddering as the tablets slipped down her throat. She rejoined the team in the incident room and headed for the whiteboard to add the information they had on the case so far. Carla joined her at the board.

"Anything surfaced yet?"

"Nothing much. Something I think we should look into is the fact that Malcolm fell out with one of his colleagues before he left the firm he was working for."

"Interesting. Okay, let's fill in the blanks on here first, and then we'll shoot over there to poke around."

Carla nipped back to collect her notebook from her desk. "Tina and Malcolm Webb, married for ten years. They had a son, Marcus, who was seven, and a daughter, Tallulah, who was five." Carla paused.

Sara glanced her way to find she had tears welling up in her eyes.

She rubbed her hand up her partner's arm. "I appreciate how tough this is. Let's set our own emotions aside and do it for the family, okay?"

Carla gulped noisily. "Yep, I hear you. Sorry."

"There's no need for you to apologise." Sara blew out a breath and asked, "Okay, places of work?"

"A factory out in the sticks for Tina, until last month, that is. They make cakes for Kipling mostly. Jordan's it's called. And Malcolm drove for M&S, delivering goods to the various outlets up and down the country. He was away from home a lot of the time. Again, he left at the end of last month to start up the steam cleaning business."

"Right, seems strange he fell out with a colleague then. I've always regarded lorry driving as a solitary occupation."

"Me, too. I suppose they get together at the depot from time to time. We'll know more when we have a word with his boss. He's expecting us in an hour."

"Good. Any news on the couple's finances?"

"They have a joint bank account with just over ten grand sitting in it. A business account was started up last week—that is showing a couple of hundred at this time."

"From work carried out?"

"Probably," Carla confirmed.

"Maybe the ten grand was a safety net for them. Perhaps they intended paying the bills for a couple of months or maybe they planned to switch the money over to the business account if it took a bit of time to take off. Either way, they weren't destitute by any means."

"Always best to have a backup plan in place when a new business is starting out."

"Relatives?" Sara asked.

"None as far as I can tell, apart from Tina's mother, Cynthia, who we met at the scene. Her husband died a few years ago of lung cancer. It would appear both Tina and Malcolm were only children. His parents died a while ago, not long after his eighteenth birthday, in a car accident."

"He's been on his own ever since. What age was he?"

"Malcolm was thirty-eight and Tina thirty-four."

Sara added the ages to the board. "Either of them been married before?"

"Not according to the records."

"But they might have lived with someone, right?"

Carla shrugged. "It's possible. Are you thinking a jealous boyfriend or girlfriend was to blame for this?"

Sara faced her partner. "We can't dismiss it, with very little else to go on."

Carla frowned. "Even though they've been married for ten years?"

"Maybe an old boyfriend has moved back to the area and wanted to rekindle a romance with Tina, or a former girlfriend in Malcolm's case. Who knows? Again, it's an angle we should look into."

They jotted down several more facts that might prove pertinent in the future such as Tina's Neighbourhood Watch duties. Perhaps she was guilty of pissing off a neighbour who didn't need a nosy parker delving into their personal business. Then they left the station and drove to the depot which serviced M&S in the area, situated around ten miles away.

The boss, Mr Parker, a man with a rotund stomach and grey hair, was in the reception area, pacing the floor awaiting their arrival. He glanced at his watch the second they walked through the front door. "You're late. I have a busy schedule to maintain. A few seconds late here and there could lose me thousands. Come through to my office, let's get this over with."

Sara and Carla followed the man through a narrow hallway to a cluttered office at the rear.

"Sorry about that, we got lost just up the road. The satnav didn't recognise the postcode for some reason," Sara said.

"Bloody satnavs are the bane of my life, leading my drivers down unnavigable narrow lanes, damn things. Take a seat."

"I'm DI Sara Ramsey, and this is DS Carla Jameson who you spoke to earlier."

"Yes, yes. Can we get on? What's this all about?"

"I take it you haven't seen the news this morning then?" Sara asked.

"Nope. I've been here at my desk since five, as usual. Our day starts early in the haulage business. You enquired about Malcolm Webb, that's as far as your sergeant went. What about him?"

"You said he'd fallen out with a colleague before he left. We'd like to speak with that gentleman, if that's okay?"

"He's on his way back from a trip up north. Why? What's Frank done? Or Malcolm for that matter? I don't have no shenanigans going on in my business. If they were on the take, I want to know about it."

"The truth is, we don't know what went on between them, that's why we need to speak to Frank Marlow."

"What's Malcolm said then?"

"Sorry to have to tell you this, but Malcolm and his family were involved in a fire at their home during the night. There were no survivors."

He flung himself back in his chair and raked a chubby hand through his thinning hair. "That's unbelievable." He sprang upright again and placed his hands on the desk. "Wait, and you think Frank has something to do with this? Why? I can't understand your logic."

"You catch on quickly, sir. We're here to ask the question, that's all. The fire was a deliberate act, and at this moment in time the only name to have surfaced in our investigation is Frank Marlow."

"I'm telling you now, there's no way he would or could have done it. Are you mad? It takes a twisted mind to fucking do something like this. Frank ain't your man, I can assure you. Anyway, he was hundreds of miles away if this fire happened last night. Yesterday he had a run to Scotland and stayed overnight. His tachograph and satnav will back me up on that, too."

Sara tutted. "If you're adamant about that then there's no point in us hanging around to speak with him. We're going to need evidence of his alibi, though."

Over Mr Parker's shoulder, a large lorry drove into the yard. He swivelled in his chair when the gravel crunched. "Ahh...here he is now. You can speak to him as long as you don't go in there gung ho. I'm telling you, there's no way he could be responsible for this. For one thing, he's a decent chap. Rest assured, he wouldn't be working here if he wasn't."

"Don't worry. Give us the evidence to eliminate him from our enquiries, and that will be the end of the matter. However, we'd still like a quick word with him. Maybe he'll be able to tell us something else about Malcolm's past that will give us a new lead."

"Such as?" he asked, standing, appearing perplexed.

"I don't know. It would be daft of us to travel all the way out here and back again without interviewing him and possibly a few other members of your staff."

Parker reached for the door handle and motioned for them to join him. "Okay, you win. Try not to disrupt the place too much. We've got a tight schedule to maintain. I'd appreciate it if you allowed my drivers to stick to that."

"Don't worry. A brief interview is all we're asking for."

Sara and Carla followed him back through the reception area and out into the cool breeze. They hung back so Parker could have a quick chat with Marlow who was unfastening the doors to his trailer. Both men looked their way for a brief moment. Then Parker gestured for them to join him.

"Can't see us getting anything out of him," Carla grumbled.

"Nope. Let's see what he has to say." When they reached the two men, Sara smiled at the new arrival. "Hello, Mr Marlow. I'm DI Sara Ramsey, and this is my partner, DS Carla Jameson. Good trip?" Sara noticed that Parker had walked away and was opening the lorry's cab door.

"Tiring. What's this about Malcolm? Is it true? That he's dead?"

"Unfortunately, yes, that's true. Do you mind if we have a quick chat with you?"

"Can it wait? I'm pooped after driving all the way from Scotland and getting caught up in the traffic on the M5."

"Not really, it won't take long."

"What are you doing, boss?" he asked Parker once he'd jumped down from his cab with the man's tacho in his hand.

"We've asked your boss to provide evidence of your trip, Mr Marlow."

"What? Why? You think I've made my trip up, is that it? Lady, I left this depot two days ago, and as you can see, I've come back empty. I have a manifest to prove where I was at every hour during the day.

What is this? Am I under suspicion for something? No! You think I had something to do with that damned fire? Are you *crazy?*" His nostrils flared, displaying how angry he was.

"Please, sir, if you'll just calm down. We're investigating an arson attack on a former colleague of yours. One who you fell out with, by all accounts. It's a line of enquiry we need to follow for now."

He turned his back and kicked out at the large tyre on his lorry. "Jesus! Boss, they can't do this to me. You're standing back as though you believe I've got something to do with this. I'm telling you, you're bloody barking up the wrong frigging tree."

"Now, calm down, Frank. I sat in my office not ten minutes ago and said the very same thing. Just let them ask their questions. Your manifest and tacho will be all the alibi you need. I don't think they're accusing you of setting the fire, they just need our help. Give them that, all right?"

Marlow heaved out a large breath and stomped his feet a couple of times. He raised a hand and pointed at Sara. "For the record, I've never even spoken to a copper in my life. Not for a speeding offence and definitely not for a bloody arson attack on a mate."

Sara nodded. "I accept what you're saying, and I must reiterate, we are not accusing you of anything. All we're trying to ascertain is what you knew about Malcolm Webb. If it's any consolation, I intend asking the other members of staff the same questions."

He shrugged. "Okay, that's made me feel better, knowing that. Where do you want to do it? I'm dying for a proper cup of coffee after my long trip."

"Do you have a canteen here?"

"Sort of. We lay on coffee, and the men bring their own food. Come on, I'll show you where it is," Parker said, heading back inside.

The four of them returned to the building, and Parker led the way into a large room filled with a cheap range of tables and chairs. In the corner of the room was a stainless-steel catering-sized urn. Alongside that, sachets of instant coffee, sugar and UHT milk cartons.

"Take a seat, all of you, I'll sort the drinks. Coffee all round, is it?" Mr Parker asked.

"That would be lovely, thank you," Sara replied.

Frank Marlow pulled out a chair and flopped into it and immediately folded his arms defensively across his broad chest. Sara and Carla both sat opposite him. Carla took out her notebook and placed it on the table in front of her.

"First of all, I'd like to ask what you and Malcolm fell out about."

"What? That was months ago."

"Just answer the question, mate. Give the inspector a break," Parker warned.

"It was nothing really. Stupid pride. He cut me up in the depot car park. Almost caused me to crash into a vehicle coming into the yard. I pride myself on driving these babies for over thirty years and never having an accident, so I blew my top."

"I see. Were there any witnesses at the time?"

"Of course there were. The other driver and a few of the mechanics saw the incident, too. They'll all tell you the same as me, that it was Malcolm's fault. All right, I shouldn't have had a pop at him, and yes, now that I know he's dead, I feel guilty about that. At the time it ticked me off, good and proper."

"Did Malcolm apologise for the mistake?" Sara asked.

"Not immediately. He had a stubborn nature at times. Found it hard to accept when he was in the wrong. Eventually he got off his high horse and admitted he was to blame."

"When he left, there was no animosity between you then?"

"No. In fact..." He glanced up at Parker standing behind Sara and paused.

"Go on," Sara prompted.

"He offered me a job. Said there would be a vacancy available by the end of the year, once he got his business up and running."

"Why would he offer an experienced driver like you a job steam cleaning?"

"I asked that very question. He told me my work ethic was second to none and he'd be on the lookout for employees who put a lot of effort into their work. I told him I appreciated the offer, but retirement is coming up in a few years. My job has its ups and downs, and the motorway traffic is driving me potty these days, but I still love the freedom of heading out on the open road at the end of the day. What the heck would I know about steam cleaning?"

"And he accepted you turning him down?"

"Yeah. What else could he do? He went on to ask several of the other drivers after that, you can ask them. Sorry, boss, not what you wanted to hear, I'm sure."

Parker grunted. "You're right. What a bloody cheek. It didn't work —no one handed in their notice."

"Did Malcolm ever mention if anyone was after him at all? If, as you say, he was stubborn and refused to back down at times, that would lead me to believe he had a strong will that could possibly lead him into trouble."

Marlow shook his head. "Nah, he never told me anything like that. He got on well with everyone mostly. The day we fell out I think he had a few things on his mind regarding the start-up of his business, as far as I can remember."

"I see. If you can't add anything further, then you're free to go. See, that was pretty harmless, wasn't it?" Sara smiled.

Marlow nodded, picked up his mug and walked away from the table.

Sara swivelled in her seat to face Mr Parker. "All right if we question the other staff while we're here?"

"I don't mind at all, especially if all the chats end as quickly as that one did. I can assure you, though, I doubt you'll get much out of anyone. To me you're wasting your time being here, when there's a killer out there you should be looking for."

"I understand what you're getting at, sir. The thing is, if we don't ask the right questions to friends and colleagues, we could be missing a trick. Something important that we wouldn't necessarily learn about otherwise. If you get what I mean?"

"All right. I'll arrange for the staff who are on site to come and see you. I'm going to get back to work, if that's okay with you?"

"Of course. Thank you for allowing us access to the staff. We'll be out of your hair soon, I promise you."

Mr Parker left the room. Sara took a sip of her coffee and mulled things over. "So, all we can glean from what we've heard so far is that Malcolm had a stubborn streak."

Carla blew out her cheeks. "Along with most men in this universe, I'd say."

Sara laughed as she thought about the men in her life—her father, brother, Mark and her brother-in-law, Donald, who definitely fit the bill on that score. "Yeah, you're right. I really thought we were onto something once we learned Malcolm had fallen out with Marlow. Best laid plans and all that."

"I was thinking the same. Not sure where we go from here. Tina was well liked in the community, did a lot for the other residents..." Carla trailed off when another driver entered the room.

"Hi, I'm Jezza. The boss told me you wanted to have a quick word about Malcolm Webb."

"That's right, Mr...?"

"Sanderson. Jeff Sanderson is my real name, sorry." He swept a stray piece of his long blond hair behind his right ear. He had a twinkle in his blue eyes, and Sara warmed to him immediately.

"No problem, why don't you take a seat? We promise not to keep you long. Did you know Malcolm well?"

"Yeah, as much as I know anyone around here. We didn't go for a drink after work, if that's what you're asking."

"But you would have done if the opportunity had arisen?"

"Without a doubt. He was a cool dude. He basically came to work, did his driving for the day then returned home to his family. He cherished his wife and kids. The boss just told me they were all lost in a fire. That's just devastating. We're all really upset about it."

"Do you recall anyone falling out with Malcolm around here?"

"No. Oh wait..." He peered over his shoulder and lowered his voice. "He had a massive argument with Frank Marlow a few months back."

"Ah, we're aware of that. Apparently, they made it up before Malcolm left the company."

"Yeah, that's right, they did. Nope, can't think of anything else. He generally got on well with the folks round here. The women all liked him, too, if you get my drift." He tapped the side of his nose.

"Are you telling me he had a flirtatious nature even though he was happily married? Or are you saying it went further than that with the women?"

"Nah, he'd never cheat on Tina, he loved and cared for her too much to damage his marriage. I suppose we're all guilty of having a laugh at work. He seemed to have the women fawning all over him. His cheeky smile and boyish good looks worked wonders."

"I see, but it never went further than flirting? We need to know, Jezza."

"No. Sorry, I shouldn't have opened my mouth. He was a decent guy who everyone liked."

"Did you ever get the impression he was faking it?"

"What? Being a nice bloke? No way. If someone's faking it, you'd see their mask slip occasionally, wouldn't you? Malcolm was as genuine as they come. Always there when you needed a chat in his shell-like. Never judged you in the slightest. He offered me a job, you know, for the new business he started up. I jumped at the chance to join up with him. I wouldn't have done that if I didn't trust the guy or thought he had an agenda, would I?"

"Was your boss aware that you were considering leaving the job here?"

He glanced at the door and leaned forward. "No. Hey, you're not going to tell him? He'd give me the sack on the spot for being disloyal."

"No, we won't tell him. Do you know how many of the other men he asked? And if they were tempted to join him?"

"He asked everyone, all except the girls in the office. Tina was going to do the secretarial side of things for him. He wanted a bunch of men he could rely on to start the business up. We've all got contacts in the trade—that's what he was relying on to get the business off the ground. Made sense to me. He was bound to succeed. Sad he's no longer with us, it's criminal. Stating the obvious, I know. I hope you catch the person responsible for wiping out that special family. I hope they can bloody sleep well in their beds at night, knowing what they've done. It's appalling."

"It is. Hopefully, we'll track the person down soon, although we're not really getting that much information that will lead us to a suspect just yet."

His mouth turned down at the sides, and he shrugged. "Sorry about that. I've told you everything I know. Maybe one of the girls' boyfriends or husbands didn't take kindly to him flirting, have you considered that?"

"We have. We'll be sure to ask the right questions when we interview the girls in the office. If you can't think of anything else to tell us, then you're free to go. Take one of my cards in case something comes to mind later."

He placed the card in his shirt pocket, smiled, then left. Two mechanics entered the room next, one after the other. They were both young and cheeky in their manner, who thought being interviewed by two pretty police officers was some kind of joke. Sara lost patience with them as soon as they opened their mouths. She had to reiterate a few times during the interview the serious nature to their questions. The men had calmed down after a while, leading Sara to believe their behaviour was born through a nervous disposition, rather than anything else.

Once they had left the room, it was time to question the two secretaries. They were both in their late twenties to early thirties.

Sara came to the point with the first secretary, Milly Jordache. "We've been told that Malcolm had a flirtatious nature. Did either you or your partner—by that I mean your boyfriend or husband—have a problem with that?"

"No, not at all. It made the day pass by quickly. Malcolm never meant any harm. I'm shocked you should think that. Why tarnish the poor man's name with untruths?"

"So, you're telling me he didn't flirt with you?" Sara asked, confused by the woman's response.

"No. He did, but it was harmless fun. No one got hurt in the process."

"I see. You work nine to five, I take it?"

Milly nodded.

"Did you ever notice anyone hanging around the yard who shouldn't have been here?"

"No, not that I can think of." Her head dipped, her chin resting on her chest. "I can't believe what's happened. Neither he nor his family deserved this."

"It is a shame. That's why we felt the need to come out here and question you all in person. We need to get to the bottom of why this event took place, and quickly. This seemed a pretty good place to start, considering Malcolm had just left his job. Do you believe that was under a cloud?"

Her head rose again, and she stared at Sara. "Not at all. He walked out of here with his head held high and everyone wishing him good luck in the future, even Frank who he'd fallen out with a few months before. Malcolm was liked by everyone. If you're saying that the fire was intentional, well, that's shocked me to the core. I couldn't conceive of anyone around here doing such a vile thing. Not in a million years."

"Thank you, that's reassuring. Here, take one of my cards. If you think of anything else we should know, please ring us straight away." Sara slid the card across the table.

"I will. Do you know when the funeral will be? I'd like to pay my respects. I think we all would."

"We're not sure yet. I'll let Tina's mother know that you were asking. I'm sure she'll be in touch nearer the time."

Milly gasped. "That poor woman, having her family wiped out in one go like that. Oh gosh, here I go again." She dabbed at the falling tears with a hanky she'd extracted from her sleeve.

"Thank you for your time. Would you mind sending your colleague in please?" Sara asked, her throat clogging up.

Milly walked out of the room, her shoulders sagging under the weight of the news.

"This isn't getting us very far," Carla stated.

"I know. We'll just interview the other secretary and go. All we've managed to ascertain so far is that Malcolm was a nice chap, a little flirtatious at times. Would those characteristics lead to someone wanting to murder him? I'm not so sure; however, we do live in a twisted world, so who knows?"

"Can't see it myself. What about the boss?" Carla asked, lowering her voice.

"What about him?" Sara tilted her head, unsure where this was leading.

"What if he did it? You know, perhaps he found out that Malcolm was trying to poach his staff. Can't see him jumping for joy over that."

Sara wasn't so sure. "Maybe. We'll make a note of it. He seemed as shocked as the rest of them when he learned about the fire."

"Maybe he's a good liar. Oh, I don't know. Just throwing it out there as nothing else has really surfaced so far."

"Quite right, too. We'll do a background check when we return to the station."

Sara looked up when the door opened and a leggy, slim brunette with long hair walked into the room. She sashayed towards them and took a seat opposite.

"Hi, is it Karen?"

"It is, Karen O'Donnell," the woman replied in a slight Irish lilt.

"Thanks for agreeing to meet with us. You're aware of what this interview is about?"

She nodded and blinked a few times as if pushing back the tears. "Yes, dreadful tragedy. Malcolm didn't deserve to go out like that, or his family. What can I do to help?" She crossed one slender leg over the other.

"Did you know Malcolm very well?"

"Not really. In passing, yes. We had a bit of banter now and again, but Milly mostly dealt with him. She's in there now, crying her eyes out, poor lass. This has really hit her hard."

"Why do you think that is?" Sara asked, intrigued.

"She liked him. Not like that. He was a genuine guy. Yes, he flirted a touch, but what guy doesn't when his missus is out of sight?"

"I suppose. Do you think there was anything going on between them?"

She slammed a hand onto the desk. Sara jumped.

"No, definitely not. Milly is in lurve with her man. He's a cage fighter, you know."

Sara turned to face Carla and raised an eyebrow. She returned her gaze to Karen and asked, "Local, is he?"

She wagged her finger, quick to cotton on to what Sara was getting at. "No way. He works up in London mostly. If you think he's the jealous type, think again."

"Good to know. Is he based in London?"

"Yes, he tends to come home at the weekends, although he had a big gig on this weekend. A sixtieth birthday event he fought at for a big knob up in the city."

"I see. Thanks for that information. We're wondering if you saw anything suspicious around the yard lately. Someone hanging around who shouldn't have been, perhaps?"

She thought the question over for a moment or two and then finally shook her head. "Can't think of anyone. We're kept pretty busy in the office, though. Heads down most of the time. Rarely have to deal with the general public. All our enquiries come in over the phone, that's what I'm trying to say."

"I see. And all the drivers get on well?"

"Yes, except for the argument that took place between Malcolm and Frank, which I believe you know about, everyone gets on really well here. If I'm honest with you, I thought there would be scraps galore with all the testosterone on show around here. I had to think long and hard before applying for the job in the first place. My dad told me I was being foolish. He used to be a haulage driver and said there is a lot of misconception about the job from outsiders."

"Understandable. Do the men make a play for you?"

"No. They wouldn't dare. My Darren would wipe the floor with anyone who tried it on with me."

"And what does Darren do for a living?"

"He's one of you lot. Only in uniform right now. He has high hopes for the future."

Sara smiled. "Wishing him every success. It's a good career to have."

"Not when there are cases like this to deal with, though, I bet."

"Some investigations are definitely harder than others, granted. Is there anything else you wish to add, Karen?"

"Can't think of anything. I'll keep my ear to the ground when you go and ring you if anything crops up, if you like? I fancy myself as a bit of a Miss Marple."

Sara laughed and passed a card across the desk. "Any help we get on this case would be a bonus."

Karen popped the card down the front of her blouse and tucked it into her bra, then stood to leave. "My pleasure. I hope some form of clue drops into your laps soon. I wouldn't like your job, too frustrating most days, at least that's what Darren says. Oops, I shouldn't have said that."

"Darren's right. Most people have the idea that police work is interesting. Seventy percent of the time it is, the rest is very mundane and, as you say, frustrating."

Karen smiled and turned to walk out of the room on her four-inch strappy heels.

Sara stretched out the knot that had lodged itself in her back. "Well, that was a waste of time. A good couple of hours we could have spent elsewhere."

Carla tucked her chair under the table and slotted her notebook into her jacket pocket. "Not sure what other leads we have to go on, so it was a no-brainer to come out here."

"You're right. Let's get back to the station, see what the team have managed to dig up so far."

CHAPTER 4

KRISTINA STONEHOUSE WAS ADDING the finishing touches to the romantic meal she was creating for her husband, Paul, to celebrate the promotion he'd just accepted. Paul had rung her at lunchtime to share the news. She'd nipped out in her lunch hour and bought all the ingredients for the slap-up meal of steak, fondant potatoes, broccoli and asparagus spears. She loved cooking for her man. He appreciated her efforts far more than any man who'd sat at her table before him.

They'd been married for seven years now and couldn't be happier. Paul's promotion up the ladder of the accountancy firm where he worked was the icing on the cake. She glanced over at the stack of travel brochures she'd collected from the agency on her way back to work. The couple enjoyed travelling. To date they had visited ten countries together from as far afield as Hawaii to one of the Greek islands which had been a magical first trip together. She'd never forget that one, but it was the more exotic locations that really thrilled her.

She smiled and wrapped her arms around herself at the thought of their next adventure— she fancied Bali but wasn't sure what Paul's reaction would be to jetting off to that location. She laughed; she knew she'd get her way in the end. Paul frequently left the decision-making up to her.

The front door closed. "Hi, love. Where are you?"

"Where I always am, in the kitchen," she called back.

He appeared in the doorway, and her heart almost stopped. She loved him deeply. Paul filled the opening with his broad frame. He wasn't carrying any excess pounds, no, far from it; he kept himself trim at the gym several times during the course of the week. He held a large colourful display of flowers.

"Wow, for me? What have I done to deserve this?"

"I just wanted to show you how much you mean to me. This promotion wouldn't have come my way if you hadn't twisted my arm to go for it. You're my rock, Kristina. You make my life whole."

A sadness crept over her where happiness should have swamped her. "Even though we can never have children? I find that incredibly hard to believe."

He strode across the floor, placed the flowers on the table and gathered her in his arms. "Why doubt it? We share a wonderful life together. So what if we can't have kids. It's not the end of the world."

Kristina sighed. To her it was. She constantly felt as if she'd failed him not being able to bear him children to continue the Stonehouse name. His mother often told her how disappointed she was that they hadn't produced a grandchild yet. She always made sure she voiced such disappointment out of earshot of her son, however. Kristina pushed aside the feelings of failure and concentrated instead on Paul's good news.

"Go and get changed. Dinner won't be long. I have a special surprise for you."

He started to walk towards the stove to see what was cooking, but she yanked him back.

"Oh no you don't. Shoo...out of my domain."

He kissed the tip of her nose. "Who am I to argue with a determined woman such as you? I'll step out in case you think of an imaginative way of attacking me with a carving knife." He ran out of the room.

She gasped and shouted after him, "Never. I could never do that to you. It would mean I'd forego all my exotic holidays in the future."

She could hear him laughing in the master bedroom above the kitchen. She smiled. Despite the disappointment of not having children, they truly had a magical marriage, rarely arguing, except possibly the once over the choice of wallpaper during the renovation the house had gone through in the past few years.

Paul reappeared, smelling of Cool Water aftershave, ten minutes later as she was dishing up the meal. Kristina was a good cook. She showed off her expertise in the kitchen at the weekend usually, when she had more time. Working full time hampered her efforts to please her man in the way she would have preferred during the week.

Working at the library was something she loved, and the job enabled them to fly around the world. Paul had tried to persuade her to go part-time, but she'd always argued against his logic. She would love to care for her man properly but valued their way of life too much to chuck it all away just to cook amazing meals every day of the week.

"Sit down. I poured you a glass of red."

"You're amazing. Are you sure I can't help?" He pulled out the chair and sat at the beautifully laid out table. The bunch of flowers had been arranged and were sitting in a vase off to the side. "It smells wonderful."

Kristina plated up the vegetables and deposited the saucepans in the sink. Happy with her achievement, she carried the plates to the table, placed his meal in front of him and bent down for a kiss. "Congratulations, Paul. I thought I'd treat you to a steak."

"Wow, no wonder it smelt amazing." He raised his glass and clinked the edge against hers. "To us and what this means to us in the future. Don't think I haven't noticed the brochures sitting on the table. Where are you thinking of heading off to this time?"

"Sorry. I know I can be predictable at times. I'll tidy up after dinner, and we'll zip through the brochures together. What about Bali?"

He laughed. "Sounds expensive. Good job I've just received a substantial raise to cover the costs."

She sipped at her wine and sliced off a slither of steak. A satisfied moan left her mouth a few minutes later. She had pushed the boat out today and forked out for a nice piece of fillet. It was worth the twenty quid she'd spent as the steak melted in her mouth as soon as she chewed it.

"Superb, love. You're a marvel in the kitchen. I appreciate your efforts."

Her cheeks warmed. "I know you do. You're worth the blood, sweat and tears it took to create the meal."

They both laughed at her exaggeration.

After they'd finished the main course, Kristina cleared the dishes away and retrieved the lemon cheesecake from the fridge.

"You didn't make that?"

She laughed. "No, Wonder Woman I am not. I cheated and bought a couple from the supermarket. Just close your eyes when you're eating it and imagine it's homemade."

"I'll do that."

The cheesecake turned out to be better than either of them anticipated. Paul took over and cleared up, loading the dishwasher for her. Kristina carried the glasses and the bottle of wine through to the lounge and returned to collect the brochures a few seconds later.

"Do you want a coffee, or shall we stick to the wine?"

"Wine all the way for me this evening, we're celebrating." She tucked her legs underneath her and patted the sofa next to her.

He joined her, and together they flicked through the pages. "This is the hotel I had my eye on. What do you think?" She covered the prices.

He tried to pull her hand away, but she held firm. "Go on then. It looks as if there is plenty to do there, and it's right on the beach. I bet the price is extortionate, am I right?"

"Maybe. We'll cut back on our other holiday, perhaps rent a cottage in the UK somewhere later on in the year. How does that sound?"

He cocked an eyebrow at her. "Really? Can you see that happening?"

She nodded. "Yes, we should see more of our beautiful country."

He placed a hand on his chest, and his eyes widened. "Wow, I never thought I'd live to hear you say that. If you're sure, then let's book it tonight."

"Let's do it at the weekend when we have more time. I hate rushing through the booking form. I'm so glad you agree with me. I think this is going to be a holiday of a life—"

The doorbell rang, interrupting her.

Paul rose from his chair and left the room. He returned with an unexpected visitor a few seconds later. The man was wearing a balaclava.

Kristina dropped her legs to the floor, sat upright and screamed. "What's going on? Who are you?" she demanded.

Paul sat on the sofa next to her, and that was the moment she realised that the man was holding a large knife. She noted it was shaking a bit. Paul grabbed her hand tightly.

"Shut up and you won't get hurt," the man warned in a gruff voice that sounded disguised.

"What do you want?" Paul asked, his voice trembling.

The intruder sat on the arm of the sofa, close to Paul, and touched the tip of the knife to his throat. "I told you to keep quiet. What didn't you understand about that warning?"

Paul swallowed. "I'm sorry. If it's money you're after we don't keep any in the house."

The man thumped his clenched fist against his leg. "I warned you."

"Ouch," Paul cried out. A trickle of blood ran down his throat where the knife nicked him.

"Please, please, don't hurt him. What do you want from us?" Kristina asked, her heart hammering.

"Shut up! That's the last time I'm going to tell you, both of you." He left the chair and walked back towards the door. He returned carrying a black holdall. He opened the zipper, slipped his hand inside and pulled out a couple of items which he placed on the carpet in front of them. One was a large hammer, the other, a petrol can.

Fear shot through Kristina. She clung tighter to her husband's hand, her gaze shifting nervously between Paul and the intruder. Neither she nor her husband uttered another word—the nick to Paul's throat had finally silenced their questions. Kristina's heart was pounding so hard her chest hurt and her breathing was becoming affected.

He made himself comfortable in the armchair on the opposite side of the room and stared at them through the slits in his balaclava, his silence the ultimate torture. His gaze drifted to the items on the floor now and again as if emphasising his point that he was in control of the situation.

They stayed like that for around an hour. "Please, I have to go to the toilet," Kristina muttered.

He stared at her, his gaze piercing into her very soul, and she shuddered. "No, you don't. Sit there."

Paul's hand clutched hers harder. "Come on, mate. What harm can it do? We consumed a few glasses of wine before you showed up. That's going to play havoc on her system."

Balaclava man was out of the chair as quick as a flash, the knife connecting with Paul's throat a second time.

Kristina screamed and then slammed a hand over her mouth.

"You two really should learn to listen to me. I hold all the cards. You're forgetting who's in charge here."

His hand shot out, and he punched Kristina in the face. She placed a hand over her mouth, suppressing her scream.

Paul shouted but remained still with the blade firmly pointed at his jugular. "Don't hurt her, please. We're prepared to do anything you ask, just please, please don't hurt us."

He laughed. "Too late for that. I warned you both to keep quiet, and you didn't, therefore, you're both going to get hurt now. Who wants to go first? You? Are you going to be the gent you've always been...?"

Paul gasped. "Do we know you? What have we done to deserve this? Why are you doing this to us?"

The man jabbed Paul's neck with the knife. He yelled and slapped a hand over the wound.

Kristina turned to her husband, and a spray of blood exploded through his fingers. "Please, no more. We'll do as you ask," she whimpered.

He laughed. "Well, it's about time. The trouble is, he's going to bleed out now. You should have followed the orders I dished out before, then this wouldn't have happened."

The couple froze in position. Kristina was tempted to take a swipe at the man but feared what he'd do with the large knife next. The man retreated a few steps and picked up one of the objects, the hammer.

Kristina gulped, a ghastly image of what the man was about to do to them playing out frame by frame in her mind. She held up a hand and whispered, "Don't do this. We've never harmed anyone in our lives, not knowingly."

The man stopped a few feet in front of them, his gaze fixed on Kristina as the hammer raised above his head. "Oh, but you did. This is payback. After tonight, you'll never be able to harm anyone else."

Paul grunted as the hammer connected with his head. He flopped against his wife, already weak from the blood loss he'd incurred. Panic rising in her chest, Kristina tried to get between her husband and the intruder. He was stronger than her and he placed one hand on her shoulder, pinning her down, while the other swung at Paul's head repeatedly. Blow after blow, the blood sprayed the room. Her vision blurred by tears, Kristina looked down at her hands covered in her husband's blood, and there was nothing she could do about it. She resigned herself to the fact that her own life would end tonight. All the fight quickly dispersed. She glanced at Paul as he took his final breath. "Goodbye, my love."

Balaclava man's manic laughter filled the room. She tried to block it out, remembering the day she had walked down the aisle with Paul, their family and friends surrounding them on the happiest day of their lives.

The next thing she knew, the intruder's covered face was inches from her own. His eyes narrowed in hatred. She closed hers, aware of what was coming her way and offered up a silent prayer to her maker.

The blows came at her fast and heavy. She felt the first blow and the second—anything after that paled into insignificance. She found the strength to wrap her arms around her dead husband. If she had been given an option of how her life would end, this would be it, with Paul right by her side. "Goodnight, my love. Sleep well."

CHAPTER 5

HE WATCHED their lives fade away. No remorse whatsoever, just like with the first family. They all deserved to die for what they had done. He placed the hammer and the knife in his holdall and emptied the can of petrol around the couple and over the chairs, assured that the fire would spread easier that way. He edged back out of the room and lit the match, throwing it on the carpet ahead of him. The flames spread quickly. He scurried up the hallway—it was important for him to leave the scene before the fire took hold.

He rushed out of the back door and up the small garden at the rear. Pulling open the gate, he bumped into a man walking his Yorkshire Terrier up the alley.

"Hey, watch what you're doing."

With the balaclava still in place, he turned to face the man and placed the knife to his throat. Sneering, he said, "You're lucky I'm in a hurry, old man, or I'd skin that rat of yours alive."

The man staggered backwards and tightened his grip on the leash. "There's no need for that. Be on your way, I've seen nothing."

"Good. Keep it that way, or I'll be back to carry out my threat. I know where you live."

The old man nodded, his eyes widening in fear.

He laughed and left the alley. At the end of it he tore off his bala-clava and returned to his car a few roads away. Satisfied by his evening's work, he started the engine and drove around the block, back to the house. The flames danced and flickered through the window of the lounge; the curtains had been stripped from the window. He grinned and drove past, not daring to slow down. A few streets away a fire engine passed him, en route to the house, he imag-ined. It didn't matter that someone had called them. He knew the occupants were dead already, he'd seen to that.

The boy done good.

Yep, we've trained him well.

After wiping off the blood spatter from his hands and face, he stopped off at the McDonald's drive-through in town, picked up a burger and a portion of fries and set off for home. He felt like a naughty schoolboy dipping into the chips during the journey. He entered the bedsit, and the first thing that caught his eye was the photo album sitting on the coffee table. He bit into his burger and stuffed a few chips in his mouth at the same time then flipped open the album.

He stopped chewing, setting his meal aside to focus on the photos of the people he loved staring back at him. The happiness leapt out of the pages, a time gone by. It was only months but felt like years since his world had ended. He traced a finger around his beautiful wife's face. They'd been childhood sweethearts until... He kissed his daugh-ter, Amelia's angelic face, her blonde curls bouncing in the breeze on that wonderful outing at the West Midlands Safari Park they'd spent the day at a few years ago.

His vision misted up. He missed them, every waking moment. Life would never be the same again, not with the gaping hole they'd left in his heart when...

He's gone off on one again. Thinking about that evil bitch and that brat of his.

Yep, he needs to get over it. He'll never get them back.

He slapped the side of his head, trying to dislodge the voices. His meal totally forgotten about, he picked up Amelia's teddy and hugged it. Memory after wonderful memory filtered into his mind. He'd been happy back then. Now his life was a sham, nothing in comparison to the joy he'd experienced with his beautiful wife, Claire, and Amelia. Nothing would ever be the same for him, ever again.

Tiredness overwhelmed him, forcing him to close his eyes. He didn't sleep much nowadays. The voices in his head wouldn't allow him to. He had to follow what they said. To carry out the awful things he'd done over the past few days. He hadn't wanted to do them. Not to end those peoples' lives. The voices had forced him. They'd also told him there would be others. People he used to know. Whom he'd mixed with at social gatherings in the past. The same people who had wronged him recently. Their punishment would come in many forms…

CHAPTER 6

Sara was settling down to an evening in front of the TV with Mark when the call came in. They ended their kiss. She was tempted to ignore the call but knew deep down that she'd never be able to do that.

"DI Ramsey. How can I help?"

"Sorry to disturb your evening, ma'am. The desk sergeant on duty told me to ring you right away, to make you aware of the situation."

Sara sat on the edge of the sofa, realising the importance of the call if the desk sergeant had told the woman on control to make contact immediately. "I'm listening. What have you got?"

"I understand you're dealing with the tragic fire that happened a few days ago."

"That's right. Don't tell me there's been another one."

"I'm afraid so, ma'am. A few streets from the other fire. This time the fire brigade managed to prevent the fire from spreading."

"Why do I sense a 'but' coming?"

"Sorry, yes, you're right. They found two bodies inside the house. Looks like they died before the fire started."

"Damn. Okay, you'd better give me the address."

"Thirty-two Frederick Street, ma'am."

"Okay, I think I know it. Can you contact my partner, DS Jameson, ask her to meet me there?"

"I'll do that now. Sorry to spoil your evening, ma'am."

"Don't worry about it." Sara ended the call and bent forward to give Mark a kiss. "Sorry, love, duty calls. Will you be okay?"

"You go. I appreciate you don't work nine-to-five. Want me to do anything while you're gone?"

She shrugged. "Apart from changing Misty's litter tray, no, nothing. Hopefully, I won't be too long."

They shared another kiss, then Sara grudgingly left the room. She yanked on her winter coat. There was a nip in the air despite it being the beginning of May. Luckily, she was still wearing her suit as she had been too lazy to change when she'd got home earlier. She slipped on her shoes and opened the front door.

"Missing you already," Mark said from the doorway to the lounge behind her.

"Don't. It's hard enough leaving you as it is. Make sure you lock all the doors before going to bed. I shouldn't be too long. Don't wait up, though."

"Shoo. Leave me to sort things out around here. I hope it's not too gruesome for you."

She closed the front door. "So do I."

Twenty minutes later, she drew up outside number thirty-two. A fire engine was still at the scene, and the firemen were in the process of storing away their hoses. She spotted the SOCO van just behind the fire engine and made her way towards it. There, stepping into her white paper suit, was Lorraine, leaning against the van for support. She glanced up when she heard Sara approach.

"Bugger me. Never expected to see you here."

"Sod off, Lorraine. Anyone would think I only attend murder scenes during daylight hours."

Her pathologist friend tilted her head. "Murder scene? Jumping ahead of yourself, aren't you?"

"Just going on the information I've been supplied by the control room. Is it wrong?"

"No. Just teasing you. Tog up, girly. I think it'll be safe for us to enter the building now these rugged, handsome creatures have done their job," Lorraine said, salivating at the firemen within close proximity of them.

"You're a pathetic flirt, has anyone ever told you that? By the way, keep your hands off the guy over there, he's Carla's new beau."

"Wow, lucky her. Tell her when she gets bored with him, I wouldn't mind a crack myself. I'd love to see the length of his hose, if you get my drift?"

Sara ran a hand over her face. "Oh dear. I don't think I'm ever going to be able to look that guy in the face now after that image filling my mind."

"Get away with you, woman. Don't get me started on the gorgeous creature you have waiting for you at home. Carla's told me what a hunk he is. Same goes for you—if you get bored of him, don't be afraid to send him my way."

Sara laughed. "You two would probably have more in common. He's more at home slicing up bodies. Slight exaggeration on my part. You know he's a vet, right?"

"I had heard. We could compare operating implements over dinner one evening."

She shook her head. "You're incorrigible. Let's get back to the task in hand, if you don't mind." Sara reached into the back of Lorraine's van and extracted a suit.

"It ain't a pretty sight, just to warn you."

"I've come to expect that lately, working the recent cases that have landed on my desk. One question: How come the fire didn't get out of control this time?"

"A neighbour called the fire brigade as soon as they saw the flames, that's what the uniform bod over there told me."

"I'll have a word with the neighbour after I've seen the scene for myself. I'm braced, let's go." She picked up a couple of blue covers for her shoes and walked towards the front door of the house.

"We're going in the back way," Lorraine shouted behind her.

Sara changed direction and headed for the alley running up the side of the house, waving at the uniformed officer who was in the process of setting up the cordon around the house. At the back door, she slipped the covers on and entered the house.

"Hey, not so fast. Wait for me. You have to allow for my age, missy. It takes me longer to get togged up these days."

"Your age or your weight? I noticed you seemed to have put on a few pounds since Christmas."

"Bit personal, cheeky bloody mare. Why do you think I'm in need of a young man?" Lorraine swiped her arm.

"Just teasing. I haven't noticed anything of the sort. Can we go in now?"

"I'm here."

Sara glanced at the rear gate. Carla walked up the path towards them.

"Sorry to call you out. I know you weren't on a date—your new fella was putting out a different kind of fire tonight."

Carla's cheeks reddened. "Crap. I wish I hadn't told you now. I knew it was too soon to blab."

"Oh, and when you're finished with him, Lorraine says she'll happily take him off your hands."

Carla flung her arms up in the air. "Is there nothing sacred between friends any more?"

Sara cringed. "Sorry. Just pulling your leg."

"She's not. I did say that. Hey, Carla, you should shout loud and proud about having a hunk like that in your bed."

Carla hid her face behind her hands and muttered, "Jesus, who the heck said I was sleeping with him?"

Sara nudged her in the ribs. "Your reaction speaks volumes, love. Come on, let's get inside."

They sloshed through the excess water sitting on the kitchen floor and made their way into the lounge. Sara gasped at the scene of the victims' faces hanging off. The woman had her arms wrapped around the man. "My guess is the man died first, the perp made her watch."

They moved closer. Inspecting the woman, she noticed patches of blood on what was left of her face and hands, either her own or her partner's. Sara took a punt most of it was the latter.

The victims' hair was missing in parts, enough for Sara to see their heads were staved in, their skulls split open to reveal their brains.

Sara gagged. "Not pleasant. I did warn you," Lorraine said, moving around the victims to get a closer look at their wounds. She pointed at the man's neck. "I think he was stabbed in the jugular, bled out slowly."

"And she was forced to watch him die? She must have been scared shitless."

Lorraine pointed at the woman's lap. "She didn't hold back."

Sara groaned and rolled her eyes. "What a callous bastard."

"That's a given, considering how he killed them," Lorraine agreed.

"Why set the fire if they were already dead?" Carla asked.

"He could have an affinity to fire. If we're dealing with the same person who killed the Webbs, that is. We've yet to have that confirmed," Sara replied, scanning the scene. She sniffed the air. "Can I smell petrol?"

Lorraine nodded. "I wondered if you'd notice. I'm getting the impression it's the same warped individual on this one."

Sara cradled her chin in her gloved hand. "Two families wiped out in a matter of days, why? The scenes are fairly close, too. Could that be significant?"

"One word springs to mind," Carla said.

"Go on."

"Actually, I should have said two. Neighbourhood Watch."

Sara went to the window and glanced out at the street. There, tied to one of the lampposts around six feet off the ground, was an orange sign. She clicked her finger and thumb. "Clever girl. What made you think of that?"

Carla shrugged. "It just struck me. It's not as if we have much else to go on, other than the knowledge that Tina belonged to the Neighbourhood Watch Scheme."

"We need to find out if this couple did. Maybe there's been a problem in the area with a gang or something lately. We need to delve into that. Can you ring the station, Carla, see what pops up in a search?"

"I'll do it now." She left the room.

Lorraine was smiling at Sara. "What?" she asked, confused.

"You two are an amazing team. She's good, you both are. Don't ever doubt yourselves as a team, Sara."

She raised an eyebrow. "High praise indeed coming from you."

"I mean it. These poor people suffered unimaginable torture before they died. We need to nail this bastard, and soon."

"Granted. It's not enough that he wiped out the Webbs, too. What gives? What motive could they possibly have?"

Lorraine snorted. "Let's face it, nowadays it doesn't take much to send someone over the edge."

Sara shuddered. "Ain't that the truth. We need to try and find an address book or something for the next of kin. I'll hunt around, if that's okay?"

"Don't envy you the task of telling the family. That part of the job I just couldn't hack."

"Yep, it's a toughie." Sara glanced around the room and walked towards the sideboard against the wall that had been untouched by the fire. Inside the third drawer she found a small pretty notebook, decorated in decoupage that appeared to be homemade. Flicking through the pages, she found an address under M, with the words *Mum and Dad*. The address was on the outskirts of Hereford in one of the outlying villages of Eardisley.

She extracted an evidence bag from her pocket and slipped the book inside. Carla entered the room a few seconds later.

"Find out anything?"

"She was part of the Neighbourhood Watch team, and no, nothing has been reported to the police from this area in the past six months. I might have something, though." She went over to the window and looked back, expecting Sara to join her. Carla pointed across the street. "Uniform told me that's the man who placed the call. The constable also said he seemed very nervous when the patrol car arrived."

"Nervous or concerned for the occupants? That would be natural if one of your neighbours' homes was on fire, wouldn't it?"

Carla shrugged. "I suppose so. Might be worth having a word before we leave. Want me to do it?"

"We'll both do it." Sara held up the small address book. "I've got the addresses of the victims' families. We'll set off soon and tell them before they hear about it on the news. First of all, I need to check upstairs, see if there are any kids in the house. I'm assuming someone has already done that, but I just want to make sure."

Carla nodded, and they left the room together. At the top of the stairs they split up. Sara headed along the hallway to what she thought was the main bedroom at the front of the house. A double bed was the dominant feature in the medium-sized room. Along one wall stood a range of built-in wardrobes, with a mixture of glass and oak doors. Matching bedside tables on either side of the bed and a chest of drawers were the only other pieces of furniture, making it seem very tight to navigate.

She stepped back into the hallway as Carla was leaving one of the other rooms. "Anything?"

"No. I searched under the bed and in the wardrobe, too. All clear. Have you checked this one yet?" Carla pointed at the next door on the landing.

"Nope." Sara followed Carla into the room. It was tiny and full of boxes, a typical spare room in any house. "That answers that then. Let's go and find out what the neighbour has to say."

They left the house, removing their suits, and crossed the street to the elderly man. He was standing, staring at the house, a small York-shire Terrier in his arms.

Sara produced her ID and introduced herself and Carla. "What's your name, sir?"

"William Randall," he replied, his gaze darting between them.

"Mr Randall, I hear you reported the fire, is that right?"

"I did. Yes."

"Thank you for doing that. You must have caught it very early, before it had a chance to take hold."

"I did. I was walking Teddy and caught the flames out of the corner of my eye. Something told me to ring nine-nine-nine at once, which is what I did."

"Thank goodness you trusted your instincts."

"What about Kristina and Paul? I haven't seen an ambulance arrive to treat them, only a SOCO van. What does that mean?"

Sara sighed. "I regret to inform you that the owners of the house, a man and a woman, were found dead inside."

The man gasped, all colour from his already pale face draining in an instant. "Oh my…I…I just don't know what to say."

"It's a shock, I know. Sir, where do you live? Maybe it would be better if we spoke in your home. You look cold and in need of a drink to warm you up."

He peered over his shoulder at a nearby bungalow. "I live there…but…"

"Is there a problem, sir? Something wrong with your house?"

He turned to face Sara again and shook his head, slowly. "No…oh my…it's just that…"

Sara reached out and placed a comforting hand on his arm. "Sir, it's obvious you're in shock. Let us take you back to your house."

Mr Randall nodded but still appeared very dazed. Sara hooked her arm through his to support him on the journey. The three of them entered the house and walked into the lounge.

"Would you like a cup of tea, sir?" Carla asked.

He nodded. "Three sugars, for the shock, please?"

Sara shook her head at Carla and mouthed, "Not for me."

She settled the old man in the worn armchair made of floral fabric which was sitting close to a gas fire. "Shall I turn the fire on, Mr Randall?"

He placed his dog on his lap, removed its leash, which he dropped to the floor, and rubbed his hands together. "It's nippier than you think out there tonight."

Sara ignited the fire and adjusted it to a medium heat. "It is, sir. Still not summer weather yet. Hopefully it's just around the corner. Are you feeling warmer now?"

"I'm getting there. Thank you, you're very kind for looking after an old man when you have such a lot on your plate."

"Nonsense, it's our pleasure. Once you've warmed up a little, perhaps you'll tell us what's on your mind?"

"On my mind? Not sure I understand." The man's brow knitted.

"I got the impression you wanted to expand on what you told us outside, Mr Randall, am I wrong about that?"

His chin dropped, and he stared at the floor by Sara's feet. "Sir?" she prompted, gently.

Carla entered the room carrying a china mug and handed it to the man. "Here you go, as you ordered it, hot and sweet."

"Thank you. You're so kind," he repeated, taking the mug in his shaking hand.

Sara and Carla glanced at each other and then back at the man who was licking his lips nervously.

Sara crouched on the floor beside him. "Sir, is there something you think we should know? Did you see someone leaving the house?"

"No. I saw no one. Don't ask me such questions," he snapped.

Sara covered his hand with hers. "I think you did. Please, if you saw who did this, you have to tell us. Do you know the person, is that it? Are you afraid to name them?"

Mr Randall tilted his head back and exhaled a breath, tears springing to his eyes. "Oh dear. God forgive me and protect me."

"Are you telling us that you started the fire, sir?" Sara asked, her own voice shaking a little as the unnerving events unfolded.

His gaze fixed on hers, and he shook his head. "I could never do that, never take someone's life. *Never.*"

"Okay, then why say what you did? What aren't you telling us, sir?"

He shook his head continuously and the threatening tears spilled down his cheeks. "I can't tell you."

"What can't you tell us? You know the person responsible, is that it?" Sara pressed, her stomach knotting into a large uncomfortable knot.

"Has someone threatened you, sir?" Carla asked.

Sara swivelled to look at her. Carla shrugged.

The man nodded. "He said he'd come back and skin my dog alive if I told anyone. There, now I've said it and put our lives in danger." He balanced his mug on the arm of the chair and hugged Teddy. "I don't want to end up a victim, neither of us do."

"I'm sorry you were put in that position. We'll protect you, I promise, both of you."

"But you're so busy. How can you protect an old man and his dog?"

Sara rubbed his arm. "Trust us, we'll do it. Do you have any family living close by?"

"No. My daughter lives up in Newcastle. I can't travel up there, not at my age."

"Will she come and collect you if I ring her and explain the situation?"

"I don't know. She's a very busy person. I really don't want to disrupt her life, become a burden."

"I'm sure she won't mind."

He shook his head. "I'd rather not bother her if it's all the same to you. I'll stay here and lock all the doors and windows."

"I'll not force you into doing something you don't feel comfortable with. I can arrange for a patrol car to drive past regularly, if that will put your mind at ease? That's the best I can do in the circumstances."

"Okay, that would be wonderful. It's the nighttime that scares me. I doubt I'll sleep much until you've caught the person."

"We can only do that if you're willing to share a description of the man, Mr Randall."

Carla took her notebook out and flipped it open beside her.

"Teddy and I were walking down the alley together on our evening walk, and a man came out of the Stonehouses' gate. He placed a knife to my throat and warned me not to say anything otherwise Teddy would be…like I already told you. I'm scared, not for me, but for Teddy. He's all I've got. He's my everything."

"I understand. Can you describe the man? Was he young or old?"

Mr Randall shook his head. "I couldn't tell."

He fell silent again. "Why? Did he have something on, a hat maybe?"

"One of them balaclava thingies, at least I think that's what they're called. Please forgive my fuzziness."

"That's a shame. Maybe you could give us a description of his build and height? That might help us further down the line."

"I'm five-eleven. I used to be six-three at one time, the joys of getting old, eh? Sorry, I digress. I would put him around the six-one or two mark. He was very lean, almost on the point of being skinny, I'd say. Dressed all in black and carrying a black holdall, he was."

"That's brilliant. Well done for having the courage to tell us. I'm going to leave my card. If you're at all worried, I want you to ring me right away. Will you promise to do that?"

"I will. Thank you, that'll put my mind at ease, a little anyway. I'm sorry I can't give you more than that."

"One last question. The man spoke to you. Did you recognise an accent at all?"

"I would say he sounded local, does that help?"

"Of course it does. It's a huge help. Is there anything you need before we go?"

"I don't think so. I'll lock up when you leave and go straight to bed."

"Good idea. Try not to worry too much. The lads on the beat will drop by throughout the night."

"Thank you. Will that be all?" He struggled out of the chair, placed his cup on top of the gas fire and rubbed at his knees. "Damn arthritis. Don't ever get old, ladies, it's a bummer."

"Nonsense, you're doing well, Mr Randall. We'll hang around while you secure the back of the house and then you can attach the chain to the front door when we leave."

He nodded and left the room, little Teddy scurrying along behind him. Sara heard the back door close, and Mr Randall returned.

"All done. I even placed a kitchen chair under the handle, no bugger will get in that way."

"Excellent. You take care. Ring me if you need assistance."

He held her card up in the air. "I will, thank you. Good luck with your investigation."

Sara smiled and turned away from the bungalow. Halfway back to the car, she fished out her phone and rang the station. The duty sergeant answered her call. "It's DI Ramsey. Can you get a patrol car to monitor Frederick Street at regular intervals, twenty-four hours a day? One of the residents was threatened by the killer."

"Blimey O'Reilly, sure thing, ma'am."

"Thanks, see you tomorrow." Sara shrugged at Carla after she ended the call. "I'll check back on Lorraine first, and then we need to pay the parents a visit."

"The fun part…not," Carla muttered as they returned to the house.

Lorraine glanced up when they re-entered the room. She stopped them coming any closer. "No suits, no access, ladies, you know the drill."

"Sorry, I must be more tired than I realised. Just a quick one before we set off. Anything else for us?"

"No, it's too soon to give you anything else. Are you going home now? It's all right for some." Lorraine grinned.

"Hardly, we're heading over to the parents to let them know. We'll swap jobs for an hour if you like?"

"No, thanks, you're the experts in that department."

"You think? Let me know tomorrow if you discover anything useful. We need to find something to get the investigation started."

"Maybe house-to-house enquiries will bear some fruit on this one."

"We're on it. The man who reported the fire was confronted and threatened by the murderer; however, he couldn't really tell us much as the person was wearing a balaclava."

"Damn, I suppose I'm not surprised to hear that."

"We're gonna take off then. Speak soon."

"Okay. Tell the parents I'll be in touch soon."

"Something for them to look forward to," Sara mumbled as she turned to leave the house.

SARA DREW the car to a halt outside a bungalow on a small estate in

Eardisley. She huffed out a relieved sigh when a light shone from the house. It was almost ten p.m. by the time Sara rang the doorbell.

Someone looked through the spyhole in the door, their eye bulbous, and Sara offered up her ID for the person to read. The door was opened by a woman in her early sixties, wrapped in a lilac velour dressing gown, which she clutched at the chest.

"Hello, Mrs Stonehouse?" Sara took a punt at the woman's surname, given that was all she had to go on was *Mum and Dad* written in the address book she'd found at the house.

"No. I'm Jane Swanley, my daughter's married name is Stonehouse. What's this about? Has something happened to my daughter?"

"Who is it, Jane? What do they want at this time of night?" a male voice came from inside the house.

"It's okay, Lawrence, I'll be with you in a moment. Be patient." She smiled tautly at them. "Is this urgent? My husband is disabled. I was just about to get him into bed."

"Sorry to interrupt you at such a late hour. Yes, it is urgent."

Mrs Swanley stepped back and opened the door to allow them access.

The bungalow was simply decorated in muted tones. In the hallway there were half a dozen doors leading off it. "Go through to the door at the end, that's the lounge. I'll collect my husband and be right with you."

Sara paced the floor in a lounge cluttered with a lot of differently styled furniture. She got the impression that the couple liked car boot sales, judging by the amount of ornaments and knickknacks sitting on every available surface.

The couple joined them a few moments later. Mr Swanley appeared older than his wife; maybe that was due to his disability.

"Hello, sir. Sorry to disturb you at such a late hour."

"What's this about? We're very concerned about your visit."

"Mrs Swanley, why don't you take a seat?"

She flopped into the armchair next to her husband. Sara and Carla sat on the sofa opposite them.

"Okay, what now?" Mr Swanley asked.

"Earlier this evening we were called out to a fire at your daughter's address..." Sara began.

"What? Is she all right?" Mr Swanley demanded while his wife clasped a hand over her mouth.

"Sadly not. When we got there the fire was out, but your daughter and her husband were both dead." Sara prepared herself for an onslaught of emotions. It was tough telling relatives the truth in instances such as this.

Mrs Swanley sobbed, and Mr Swanley stared at Sara in disbelief. "Are you sure?"

Sara nodded. "Yes, sir. I know this has come as a shock to you both, there was no easy way of telling you. I'm sorry. Can we get you a drink?"

Mr Swanley wheeled himself over to a sideboard on the other side of the room and yanked open the door. He extracted two tumblers and filled them both with amber liquid. Sara leapt out of her seat to help him.

He handed her one of the glasses. "Give that to Jane, please. She needs it." He stored the bottle away again and returned to his position next to his wife. "Drink up, love. It'll help ease the shock."

His wife sipped at her brandy and shuddered as the liquid slipped down her throat. "How... how did the fire start? Kristina is usually so careful around the house."

"It wouldn't have mattered how careful she was, it was started deliberately. I regret to have to tell you that your daughter and her husband were both killed before the fire started."

"What? How do you know that?" Mr Swanley asked, taking a large gulp of his drink.

"Your daughter and her husband both had fatal injuries that weren't caused by the fire."

Mr Swanley gripped his wife's hand. "Who would do such a thing? Our daughter, I mean they both were decent, caring people. The sort who would avoid any form of conflict."

"By that I take it that neither of them had fallen out with anyone in recent weeks?" Sara asked, a sense of frustration settling over her.

"No, never. God, we'll never see her again...I can't believe this. What a waste." Mr Swanley's voice was quaking under the strain.

Sara got the impression he was trying to hold back his feelings for his wife's sake. "Our investigation has only just begun. I wish I had some answers for you. The truth is, I haven't. Not right now."

The couple shook their heads, shocked by what they were hearing. Mrs Swanley finally broke down and sobbed.

Her husband wheeled himself closer to her chair and flung an awkward arm around her shoulder. "There, there, love. Let it out."

"My poor baby. Murdered in her own home," Mrs Swanley whispered between sobs.

"Don't dwell on that aspect. It'll be easier if you don't. Think of Kristina as she was, always happy and full of joy..." Mr Swanley himself broke down and was unable to continue.

Sara's throat clogged up, like it usually did when she had to share such bad news, her own tragic circumstances toying with her emotions. "Would you like us to contact another member of your family to come and be with you?"

Mr Swanley shook his head. "Kristina and Paul were our only family. Now they're gone, we have no one. Only each other."

"I'm sorry to hear that. Look, we don't want to keep you any longer than necessary. Would you like us to call back another time?"

"I'd rather you hunt down this evil person, the person who has robbed us of our beautiful child."

"We'll be doing our best to do just that, I promise you. There are a few more questions that I need to ask, but we can do that in the next day or two, if you'd prefer."

"No. We'd much rather get it over and done with. What do you need to know? We'll do our best to answer your questions," Mr Swanley responded, swallowing hard.

"Perhaps you can tell us where your daughter and her husband worked?"

"Kristina worked at the library, the main one in town. She's been there for around sixteen years, loved her work. Paul..." Mr Swanley paused to take a breath. "He's just had a promotion. Kristina rang us earlier today to tell us. They were both excited about it. She was cooking him a special meal tonight to celebrate the good news."

"Oh dear. Where did Paul work?"

"Sorry, I should have said, my mind is…he worked at Halshaws, the accountants. One of the directors had retired, and Paul was working his way up the ladder. They had everything to live for, and now…" He ran a hand over his face as fresh tears surfaced.

Sara glanced at Carla, at a loss what to say next.

Carla took the hint to help her out. "Is that in Hereford, Mr Swanley?"

"Yes, that's right. They've been around for years. Why do you want to know?"

"It's a matter of course. We'll go to their places of work and ask the same questions. Maybe someone there can tell us if either your daughter or her husband had any problems with one of their colleagues or a member of the public they've come into contact with lately," Sara replied, managing to suppress her emotions.

Carla went back to taking down some notes.

"Well, I hope they can tell you something that we can't."

"I don't suppose you have Paul's parents' address handy? We'll need to visit them, let them know what's happened."

"He only had his mother, she lives over in Ireland. I doubt you'll want to travel that far."

"Ah, no, that won't be possible. I'll contact the local station and get them to notify her."

Mr Swanley wheeled across the room to the sideboard, opened one of the drawers and extracted an address book. "We don't have much to do with her really, only send her a Christmas card every year. She does visit Paul regularly, at least she did. She's going to be devastated, more than that. Her husband died of liver cancer a few years ago. She's been lost ever since his death."

"That's very sad. Does she have other relatives nearby over there?"

"I believe she has a sister who lives a few streets away."

"I'll inform the police in Ireland of that, let them make arrangements for someone else to be there when she's told. Either way, it's going to be hard for her to handle, I suspect."

Mrs Swanley blew her nose. "It's hard for all of us. It still hasn't sunk in yet. Why? Why would someone kill them? For what reason? That's what I can't get my head around."

"All I can say is that this is the second fire we've had to deal with in the past few days."

"What? Here, in Hereford?"

"Yes, unfortunately the other fire involved a whole family, two adults and two children."

Mrs Swanley gasped. "Oh my, that poor family. And that was a deliberate act, too?"

"Yes, that's all we know at present. The fire investigation team are going over the scene now. Until we have the report from them, we can't go any further." She thought about asking the couple if they knew the Webbs but reconsidered that swiftly, not wishing to upset them further.

"Two fires in a matter of days? Why would anyone do that? I've always thought it would be a horrible way to die." Mrs Swanley covered her face with her hands and sobbed until her shoulders shook.

Sara was dying to leave now. She'd had her fill of emotional turmoil in the last few years, and seeing the couple so upset was bringing everything flooding back. It was the hardest thing in this life for someone to deal with, a member of their family being murdered. She should know.

Instead, she and Carla remained with the couple, sharing their grief for the next thirty minutes. At one point, Sara had nipped out into the hallway to place the call to Ireland and instructed someone with tact to go and visit Paul's mother to share the fateful news.

Eventually, Sara made their excuses and left the bungalow, telling the couple to ring her if they needed any questions answered or help with any other matters that should crop up to do with their relatives' deaths.

She glanced at her watch; it was almost eleven p.m. "Don't know about you, but I'm cream-crackered and ready for my bed. Why don't we call it a night and continue this tomorrow?"

Carla agreed and waved as she got in her own car and left the scene.

Twenty-five minutes later, Sara let herself into her home and secured the door behind her. Misty ran down the stairs to greet her. In the distance, voices babbled on the TV that was still on in the lounge. With Misty in her arms, she poked her head around the door to find Mark asleep on the sofa. She watched him breathing deeply for a few moments and wondered if he was reliving the torture he'd endured whilst dreaming. The torture he'd suffered at the hands of the gang only because he was associated with her.

His breaths became more and more erratic. She placed Misty on the floor and crept into the room, perched on the arm of the sofa and touched the top of his head, gently combing back a clump of hair that had flopped over his eyes. He flinched and opened his eyes immediately.

"Hey, it's only me. You were having a dream."

He sat upright and ran his hands through his hair. "A nightmare more like. Will they ever end?"

She dropped onto the sofa beside him and placed a hand on his thigh. "Why didn't you tell me you'd been having nightmares?"

He pushed her hand away and jumped off the sofa. "Why? What could you possibly do about them?"

Sara frowned. It was totally unlike Mark to raise his voice at her. She was perplexed by the confusion etched into his features. "Mark, don't do this. Speak to me, don't shut me out or accuse me of something I haven't done."

He paced the floor a number of times and then headed for the door. "I'm going to bed."

Misty jumped onto her lap and rubbed her head under Sara's chin. She stroked her cat, her thoughts remaining on Mark and the turmoil he was going through. She knew what he needed. The trouble was, she had a feeling he was about to decline any help she was willing to give him. He'd changed since he'd returned home. Some days he was perfectly fine, his old self, and sometimes he bit her head off the instant she opened her mouth.

How in God's name was she going to broach the subject about him seeing a counsellor? Even she had rebelled against the idea when she'd lost Philip; however, her DCI at the time in Liverpool had been proved right—it was what she'd needed to enable her to get her life back on track. Mark needed the same to ease what he was going through.

She let Misty out to do her business and stood at the back door, staring up at the stars in the chilly clear night. It had been a long day. She could do without the anxiety trickling through her veins but it was obvious Mark needed help.

"Come on, girl, in you come." Misty shot past her into the house, and Sara locked the back door. Then she returned to the lounge, switched off the TV and ascended the stairs on weary legs. Her head was thumping with the start of a headache taking its toll. Mark was sitting upright in bed, his chest bare, reading the latest thriller he'd bought. He glanced up, his watery eyes connecting with hers.

"I'm sorry. That was uncalled for. I don't know what came over me."

She crossed the room and sat on the edge of the bed next to him. "I do. Mark, you're going to have to admit you need help. By that, I mean professional help to deal with what you're going through."

"I can't do it. A counsellor will expect me to go over things, time and time again. I don't want to keep reliving what they did to me. All I want to do is forget about it and move on with my life, our life together. It's harder than you think."

She held his hand. "I know how hard it is, I went through the same when Philip was murdered. Honestly, it'll do you good to speak to an outsider. Someone who knows nothing about you. You need to let your feelings out. It's the only way you're going to get through this, love, believe me. Let me make an appointment for you, please?"

He inhaled and exhaled four deep breaths before he finally nodded his approval. "If you think it will help, then I suppose there's no harm in seeing someone for a session or two."

He leaned forward and kissed her on the nose. "I'm so lucky to have met you."

She shook her head. "If you hadn't met me you wouldn't be dealing with all this crap. This is down to me. I'm so sorry you're going through this shit."

He pulled her into his arms. "Together we'll get through it. Be patient with me, that's all I ask. Remember how much I love you. I sense there will be testing times ahead for us both."

"Let's make a pact to overcome them together, how about that?"

"Deal. Now, are you coming to bed?" he asked, a twinkle glittering in his eye.

"Two minutes, I just need to brush my teeth."

He grinned. She left the bed and looked back over her shoulder at the door to the en suite. He was smiling. *She* was the lucky one to have him in her life.

CHAPTER 7

THE FOLLOWING DAY, Sara arrived for work at her normal time. Carla was already there. "Did you get any sleep last night?" she asked her partner.

"Not much. You?"

"Fell asleep as soon as my head hit the pillow for a change. Maybe I'd be better off doing seventeen-hour days to help me sleep at night."

"Don't expect me to sign up for that."

They both laughed. Carla headed for the vending machine while Sara marched into her office to see what tripe awaited her there in the form of paperwork. Carla deposited a cup of coffee on her desk as she slipped off her jacket and placed it on the back of her chair. "I'll be out when the rest of the gang are here. Until then, I'll be knee-deep in this shit."

"I'll leave you to it. Want me to bring the whiteboard up to date with the latest incident and the information we've managed to glean so far?"

"That would be great, except we don't have much more than the victims' names, do we? Ignore me, I should be looking on the bright side, except I can't seem to think of any positives that have struck me about the investigation so far. We're up the proverbial creek on this one in my opinion."

"We should be used to that by now. It's still early days. Did you catch the snippet they mentioned on the news last night?"

"No, I went straight to bed when I got home. What did they tell the public?"

"They mentioned that two fires had taken place this week and that the fire crews had been busy in the same area of the city."

"Harmless enough, I suppose. I'll get in touch with the media circus once we know more. At the moment, I can't really tell them much."

"We'll see if we get any phone calls from the story they ran. As it stands, there's nothing to report on that front."

Sara flopped into her chair and tucked it under her desk. "So what's new? I won't be long."

Carla took the hint and left her to it. The next forty-five minutes consisted of opening her internal mail, most of which had been repeated over the past few weeks. Head office had a habit of ensuring their staff read every letter, often sending out the same letter at least three times. The latest entailed a change in a procedure that she had fought hard to achieve with DCI Price. She smiled, relieved that folks higher up the food chain were finally listening to the cops dealing with the general public, at the heart of policing the streets of Hereford.

She completed her task and joined the rest of the team in the incident room. "Okay, I see Carla has brought the boards up to date. Here's where we stand: we have two reported arson attacks within a few streets of each other. The second one was far more sinister than the first, in my eyes. The victims, Kristina and Paul Stonehouse, were savagely attacked by the arsonist before the fire was started. Did something go wrong? Or was it his intention to start a slower burning fire with the specific aim of sending us a message about the victims? I'm not sure. Or it could have been that a neighbour was quick to react and call the fire brigade the second he witnessed the flames. Either way, the Stonehouses were already dead before the fire took hold. We've yet to get the PM report back on the first fire, so we don't know if the family were killed before the fire was started or not. It's all very puzzling. The main problem for us is that we have a murderer on the loose with what appears to be some kind of agenda. What that agenda is, well, that's the biggest puzzle of all. We don't have enough clues to go on to help us form a solid picture at this time. Carla, why don't I leave it up to you to tell the team what your idea was at the scene yesterday?"

"I had an inkling that this has to do with both areas being in the Neighbourhood Watch Scheme. I don't have any more than that, except that Tina Webb was involved in the scheme and helped her neighbours out a fair bit. We've yet to discover if the Stonehouses were into all that."

"Which is why I think we need to get out there and start pounding on the doors of the neighbours. I don't want to leave the house-to-house enquiries to uniform in case they miss something vital. I know you guys won't let me down. So that's what we're all going to do, get out there and walk the streets. Jill, I need you to remain here to man the phones. Carla said the media ran a short story last night. Maybe we'll get some calls regarding that feature."

"Will do, boss. Want me to continue the searches into each of the victims' background? I must admit, nothing valuable has shown up thus far. I still need to run the last victims through the system, though."

"You do that. Carla and I are going to venture out to their places of employment after this meeting is over. Maybe something will turn up there."

Next, Sara split the group into teams and assigned them each an area in which to conduct their enquiries, with strict instructions to contact her the second they found out anything they felt was significant.

The team set off, including Sara and Carla who took Sara's car to the accountancy firm where Paul Stonehouse had worked. Halshaws was located down a side street off the main shopping area in Hereford.

A lady in her fifties sat behind a small reception desk. She looked up from her computer and smiled. "Can I help?"

Sara flashed her ID at the woman. "DI Sara Ramsey and DS Carla Jameson. We'd like to speak to the person in charge if that's possible?"

"I think Mr Jewell is free at present. I'll be right back."

The woman shuffled up the narrow corridor. It looked like she had something wrong with her leg. The receptionist returned and beckoned them up the hallway. They entered a large room, and standing behind the desk was a tall, heavily built man with grey wispy hair. His brow creased with concern. The receptionist introduced them.

"Please, take a seat," Mr Jewell requested.

"It's kind of you to see us at short notice, sir."

"What's this about, Inspector?"

"One of your employees, Paul Stonehouse."

"Ahh, he's not here today. No doubt he went overboard with the celebrations last night regarding his long overdue promotion."

Sara shook her head. "We've heard he was promoted. The thing is, well…last night we were called out to an incident at Mr Stonehouse's home and…"

"And what? What are you trying to tell me, that Paul was involved in an incident at his home?"

"Unfortunately, both he and his wife were killed last night."

The man's eyes widened, and he swallowed hard. "What? They're dead? How?"

"They were murdered."

He placed the heel of his hand in the centre of his forehead and screwed it from side to side. "Jesus…I can't believe what I'm hearing. He was only forty, had his whole life ahead of him, they both did. Good Lord, what would possess someone to kill a gentle man like Paul? Why? To achieve what exactly?"

"We've yet to find that out. What we need to ask you is if Paul has had any problems at work lately, either with clients or with other members of staff perhaps."

"No, nothing that has come to my attention. Paul was the easiest-going chap around. Always bending over backwards to help people.

You can ask the rest of the staff, I'm sure they'll all say the same. My God, what is this world coming to? Did an intruder get into their house? Was it a robbery gone wrong?"

"We can't say anything further, I'm afraid, not because we don't want to, we just don't know. The couple were killed before the perpetrator set fire to their home."

"To hide the fact they'd been killed, is that it?" He shook his head, and his gaze darted between her and Carla.

"We think that's probably what happened."

"Anything we can do to help, you only have to ask."

"Thank you. All we need to try and ascertain is whether someone had a grudge against Paul."

"No, I'd never believe that, not of him. You couldn't be more wrong to think that, Inspector."

"I have a feeling you're right; however, it's something we need to consider. Would you mind if we spoke to the other members of staff? Maybe they're aware of something that has slipped past you."

"Of course. There are four others who work here. We're a small firm, more intimate with our clients. Oops, that didn't sound right."

"I know what you mean."

"Let me gather them together in the staffroom. I'm sure they'll be just as shocked as I am to hear the news."

"Thank you."

He left the room and returned to collect them both within a few minutes. He led the way to the back of the property. Four sombre faces stared at them as the three of them entered the staffroom.

"These police officers would like a word with each of you. Please, try and help them as much as you can. We need to assist the police to apprehend who did this to poor Paul and his wife. A time when they should have been rejoicing in life."

"Thank you, Mr Jewell. Did anyone here know Paul well enough for him to confide in them?" Sara asked.

A small woman dressed in a grey pin-striped skirt suit raised her hand. "We shared an office for a while. I suppose I know Paul better than anyone else present."

"Thank you. Can we have a word privately in that case?"

"In my office?" the woman suggested. She gestured for Carla and Sara to join her as she led them back to the front of the property. She pushed open a door that revealed a smaller room than Mr Jewell's.

"Sorry, I didn't catch your name?" Sara asked, sitting in one of the spare seats in front of the desk.

"Penny Calder. I'm an accountant here."

"Have you worked with Paul long?"

"Over seven years. He was a sweetheart. I'm shocked to hear he's no longer with us. He doted on his wife, Kristina. They had a very strong bond, much stronger than any other couple I know."

"It is very sad. Is there anything out of the ordinary that has happened which you think we should be made aware of? Did Paul mention if he'd fallen out with a friend, anything along those lines? Did he hack off a client perhaps?"

"No, nothing. He had a happy home life; not sure he had many friends as such. He always preferred spending time with Kristina. He mentioned attending the odd function now and again out of a sense of duty to appease his wife. But he always insisted that if the world stopped spinning tomorrow, as long as he was with his wife Kristina when it ended, he'd be happy." She swiped at a tear that escaped her eye.

"That's lovely. Such a tragedy that's how his life ended. At least they were there to support each other come the end." Sara thought back to the way Philip had died in her arms after the shooting. To be there when he'd taken his last breath was a bittersweet moment. Looking back on it now, she wouldn't have had it any other way. "I have to ask if he's ever mentioned if his wife had any problems. Not her personally, but perhaps with someone else making a nuisance of themselves? We're struggling to find a motive, you see."

"No. Paul only ever spoke about his wife in a positive way. In my eyes they truly were the perfect couple. Most people strive to have a happy relationship with their partners. Very few people actually achieve it, especially nowadays, with our disposable culture. If a relationship isn't working out then that's it, people up and leave and don't tend to look back."

"That's very true. Okay, I think now we've got a clearer picture of the couple. Thank you for sparing us the time today."

"Do you have any idea when the funerals will be? I think we'll all want to pay our respects."

"We can't say at the moment. The post-mortems should be carried out in the next day or two. It'll be up to the pathologist to release the bodies, depending on the results. I'm sure the family will be in touch with the arrangements." Sara stood and shook the woman's hand.

"Let's hope you find the person who carried out the attack soon. It makes me shudder to think there are such evil people walking our streets."

"We're doing our best. Goodbye." Sara left the room and walked back through the reception area with Carla a few steps behind her, not sensing it necessary to have a word with the others who hadn't known Paul very well. "We'll be off now," she told the receptionist. Maybe she would be the exception to Sara's thinking. "A quick question before we go. You're probably aware by now that Paul Stonehouse lost his life last night, along with his wife."

The receptionist nodded, her expression one of sadness.

"I don't suppose you've noticed anyone hanging around outside, looking suspicious, or have dealt with a strange phone call that you put through to Paul in recent weeks?"

The woman sighed and entwined her fingers on the desk. "No, nothing at all. He was such a nice chap, they both were. We'll miss Paul around here. He brightened up the place every time he entered a room. It's sad to think we'll never get the chance to say goodbye to him properly."

Sara sighed. "Okay, thanks very much for your help."

They left the building, dejected. Sara didn't speak again until she was sitting in the driver's seat. "This case is making my heart ache." She slammed her fist onto the steering wheel and leaned her head back against the headrest. "Why? Why hurt these innocent people like this? From what we've gathered so far, they were a couple of good guys. What possible harm could they have done to someone to make them so angry as to want to murder them? None of this makes sense, or am I missing something?"

"I have the same questions running through my mind. You're right, it doesn't make sense. But then, half the cases we investigate are puzzling to begin with until the clues start to float to the surface. We've just got to keep digging, asking the right questions. Something is bound to come our way sooner or later, it has to."

Sara nodded and slipped the key into the ignition. "I hate being frustrated and feeling a failure."

"Whoa, you can cut that out. We're not failing anyone, not yet. It's only been a couple of days since the first fire. Until we get the reports from the fire investigation team and the PMs our hands are tied. We're doing the right thing, questioning loved ones and friends for now. It's all we can do."

"I know. Just ignore me, my impatience is prominent, that's all. Next stop, Kristina's place of work."

Ten minutes later, they were standing in the large library waiting at the reception desk to be seen by one of the three librarians on duty, dealing with the customers in the small queue. Sara had her ID in her hand, ready for when it was their turn to be seen. One of the older librarians smiled and came towards them.

"Hello, what can I do for you?"

Sara showed her ID and said quietly, "DI Sara Ramsey, and my partner, DS Carla Jameson. Is the person in charge available please?"

The woman, her half-rimmed glasses perched partway down her nose and her beehive standing tall, frowned. "The police? Yes, I'm in charge. Miss Davidson. Would it be better if we went to my office?"

"That would be great, thank you."

The woman spoke to her associates and then pointed to the end of the reception desk where Sara and Carla met up with her again. She led them to an office a few feet away and instructed them to take a seat. She removed her glasses when she sat and smiled warily. "How can I help? It's not often the police come knocking on our door, so to speak."

"We're here about Kristina Stonehouse."

"You are? Oh my, she hasn't been in an accident, has she? I've tried to ring her off and on all morning and I haven't received an answer on either her mobile or her house phone. She was due in today."

"I'm sorry to have to tell you that Kristina and her husband both died last night."

Miss Davidson's mouth gaped open. She shook her head in disbelief and placed a shaking hand on her face. "What? How?" she managed to utter after a little while, her voice shaking.

"Unfortunately, they were murdered in their own home."

"No!"

"The investigation is in its infancy, but we're trying to ascertain if either of them had any enemies or had fallen out with anyone recently."

"No, I don't believe Kristina ever had a bad word to say about anyone. They were a lovely couple. This beggars belief."

"What about problems with one of your customers?"

"No, never. We may get the odd person who likes to spout off, but basically everyone we deal with is pretty friendly."

"I see. And you haven't spotted any strangers hanging around outside, possibly watching the staff members?"

"Not that I can recall. Like a stalker, is that what you mean? You think someone took a liking to Kristina and followed her back to her house?"

"It's a possibility that we need to investigate."

"I can't say I've noticed. Is no one safe these days? They were an adorable couple who wouldn't have hurt a fly. Devoted to each other and making each other happy, such a rarity in today's society. It's shocking!"

"Maybe we can speak to the rest of the staff, in case they're aware of an issue that you don't know about."

"Of course. They'll do anything to help. Let me bring them in."

Sara smiled as the woman left her seat. "We'd prefer to see them one at a time if that's okay?"

She exited the office and returned with another female member of staff. Sara questioned the woman, but it proved pointless. She had the same result with the next lady she spoke to. Deflated, she asked the final woman the same question. Miss Lancaster sat in her boss's chair.

"Yes, there was an incident a few weeks ago with a homeless man. He'd set up camp outside on the steps. We drew straws as to who was going to speak to him, and sadly Kristina drew the short straw."

Carla whipped out her notebook and took down the details.

"Can you tell us what happened?" Sara asked, her heart thumping.

"Kristina went outside. I stood by the door in case the man kicked off. She asked him politely to move on, but he refused. So she threatened to call the police. The man started shouting abuse at her. I have to say, it was quite unnerving for both of us. Kristina remained strong and didn't back down, whereas I would have. Eventually the man grumbled his discontent but gathered his things and left. Kristina gave him an address of a hostel to try. He seemed grateful for that and wished us both a good day before he went on his way."

Sara's shoulders slumped in disappointment. What could have possibly been a good lead had just fallen flat on its face. "So the man left without causing any more hassle?"

"Yes. Kristina felt sorry for the man. I know I should have, too, but he smelt terrible. I know that's not his fault, but that's what I'm trying to get across. To Kristina it didn't matter. Yes, she was keen to move the man on to pastures new, but how many other people would have thought to give him the address of a nearby hostel to try? There's another thing—I thought I saw her slip the man a tenner at the same time."

"That was kind of her."

"I didn't mention that I'd seen her do it because I presumed she wanted to keep it a secret. That's the type of person she was, kind and considerate at all times. I can't believe she's gone."

"It's very sad. Thank you for sharing that with us. I'll leave you my card. If you think of any other incidents that might have occurred in recent weeks or months, will you contact me?"

"Of course. I'll do anything I can to help you find the person who did this."

"Thank you."

The three of them returned to the reception area. Sara dished out a few more cards to the other librarians and bid them all farewell.

"I can't help thinking we're wasting our time," Sara announced as they walked around the side of the building to the car.

"It's a necessary evil at this stage. We're desperate for a break. Maybe the team are faring better on the house-to-house stint."

"Possibly. I need cheering up. I'm going to stop off at the baker's and treat everyone to lunch."

"Let me go halves with you. You're always thinking of others, you have bills to pay, too," Carla insisted.

"Once in a blue moon doesn't hurt. You keep hold of your money."

Sara drove to Gregg's and picked out a variety of sandwiches and cakes and hopped back in the car. She deposited the carrier bag on Carla's lap. "That should do."

"Blimey, how many are you intending to feed? The whole station?"

"OTT?"

"And some."

They hadn't been back at the station long when Sara received a call from the hospital. Carla patched the call through to her office where she was eating lunch. "Hello. DI Sara Ramsey. How can I help?"

"Hello, Mrs Ramsey. I'm Geraldine, a nurse at the Accident and Emergency Department at Hereford County Hospital."

"Yes, what can I do for you?" Her heart was racing, and her breath caught in her throat.

"I have some bad news for you, I'm afraid."

CHAPTER 8

"WHAT IS IT?" *Oh no, don't tell me Mark has had an accident in the oper-ating theatre at work.*

"Your parents were involved in an accident a while ago. They've been rushed in for emergency care."

"What? No! Are they okay?"

"Please, I don't want to worry you any more than necessary. Is there any chance you can come to the hospital? We'll tell you more when you arrive."

"I'm on my way. Please, just tell me they're alive?"

"They are. Drive safely. Report to the receptionist, she'll call me straight away."

"Thank you, see you soon." Sara slipped on her jacket, dumped the rest of her sandwich in the bin and rushed out of the room. "I have to get to the hospital. It's my parents, they've been in an accident. Carry on, guys. I'll report back when I can."

"Sara, let me drive you. You're in no fit state to," Carla insisted.

Sara nodded. Her mind was full of bad scenarios. She doubted she'd make it to the hospital in one piece if she drove herself.

They flew down the stairs and out to the car. She remembered Carla touching her leg a few times during the journey, checking to see if she was okay, but she was too wrapped up in her own traumatic world to reply. *Let them be all right. I'm not ready to say goodbye to them yet.*

During the journey, Sara placed two calls. The first one to her sister, Lesley, who was devastated by the news and promised she would get to the hospital as soon as she could as she was in Birmingham on a course for work for the day. She did ask Sara to keep her informed regularly with updates. The second call was to her brother, Timothy. He was also away on a work function for the week, this time down in Devon. Sara told him not to fret and to stay there, and that she would ring him if she felt it necessary for him to come home early. This heaped yet more responsibility on her shoulders.

Carla slotted into a space in the car park closest to the main entrance, and they ran the short distance and entered the building out of breath. "It's this way."

Sara nodded and tried to calm her breathing as they swept through the clinically white corridors to A&E. "I received a call from a nurse called Geraldine, is she here?" Sara asked the receptionist.

"One minute, I'll get her for you. Have a seat."

Sara shook her head. "I'm all right here. Please, hurry."

The receptionist left her desk and rushed down a corridor behind her. She returned a few seconds later with a nurse who had a smile fixed on her face.

"I'm Geraldine. I'm so glad you could get here so soon. Come with me."

Sara trotted after her while Carla remained in the reception area. "Please, tell me how they are. I can't bear not knowing."

"Your mother is doing well. I'm taking you to see her now. Your father is not so good, I'm afraid."

"Why? What's wrong with him?"

"Let's get you in to see your mother first, and then I'll get the doctor to come and see you both to explain what's going on with your father."

Tears pricked her eyes. "That sounds ominous, as though you don't expect him to live."

"It would be best if he filled you in. Your father's situation is diffi-cult because of his heart."

"I knew it. He's been under the specialist for a while."

The nurse smiled and nodded. "We're aware of that. Here we are." She drew back a curtain to reveal Sara's mother.

"Oh, Mum, look at you. You've been in the wars. Are you okay?" She ran to hug her mother and kissed her bandaged forehead gently.

Her mother reached for her hand. "It was terrible, Sara. One minute your father and I were chatting, and the next, it was as if he left me, was in a world of his own. That's when we hit the tree. I don't think he saw it. I'm all right, escaped with a few cuts and bruises. I need to know what's going on with him, and they won't tell me."

"We're doing our best to get him comfortable, Mrs Ramsey, please bear with us. We're doing our best. I must get back, they need me."

The nurse drew the curtain around the bed again.

Sara sat on the chair next to her mother. "I'm so sorry you had to go through this, Mum. Let's not think negatively about Dad, he's in safe hands. They hinted it might be his heart."

"I'm not surprised. I think he might have had a heart attack, love."

"Oh Lord! I hope you're wrong about that. Where were you going?"

"Ironically, to pick up his prescription from the chemist. We'd got what we needed and were on our way back home when it happened. All I could think of was that we were both going to die. Thankfully, your father doesn't drive very fast nowadays, not like he used to. Otherwise I don't think we'd be here now. Let's hope it's not as serious as they're making it out to be."

"I'm sure we'll find out soon enough, Mum. What a scary thing for you to go through. I'm glad you're not too badly hurt. You should heal quickly."

"I might heal quickly; whether I'll ever get in another car is a different story."

"Mum, that's a daft thing to say, considering you live out in the sticks."

"I'll move closer to town rather than sit in another damn car."

"We'll talk about this later, after we find out how Dad is. This will all blow over soon."

"Maybe, but I'll never forget what happened. You're lucky, you've never been in an accident, love. It's traumatic. Look at me! Who would have thought I'd be sitting in a hospital bed at my age due to an accident? Not me, that's for sure."

"Let's discuss it another time. An accident can occur to anyone, Mum, at any age."

"I'm well aware of that. Stop treating me like a child, Sara."

"I wasn't." She stood and kissed her mother's cheek.

"I'm sorry for snapping. I'm concerned about your father."

The curtain rustled, and a young doctor appeared. "Hello, I'm Doctor McNally. I've been assessing your husband, your father."

"Good to meet you, Doctor. What can you tell us?" Sara asked.

"Unfortunately, your father suffered a heart attack, which undoubtedly caused the accident. We're moving him to Intensive Care. They'll monitor his progress there. Reading his notes, he's had problems with his heart over the past year or so. There's been talk of a heart bypass from what I can see can see. We'll have to see how he goes over the next few days. That bypass may be brought forward, depending on his recovery."

"Is he conscious?" her mother asked.

"No. We're keeping him sedated for now, letting his body heal itself before we reassess what needs to be done. His vital signs are not quite where we'd hope them to be at this point. We'll keep a close eye on him over the next few days."

"Thank you for letting us know. Can we see him?"

"Soon. Let's get him settled in ICU first. How are you feeling, Mrs Beaumont?"

"I'm fine. A little sore but concerned about my husband."

"Which is understandable. We're going to keep you in overnight for observation. We're waiting for news on a bed in the women's ward. Shouldn't be too long now. I'll check back on you shortly."

"Thank you, Doctor." Sara wanted to bombard the doctor with questions. She would have, too, if her mother hadn't been present. But she really didn't want to cause her mother any more anxiety than was necessary.

The doctor left. Sara turned to face her mother to see tears rolling down her face. Her throat closed up as she hugged her mother and reassured her that everything was going to be okay.

After a while, her mother ran out of tears and fell asleep sitting up in bed. Sara grasped the opportunity to go back to the reception area to let Carla know what was going on.

"Gosh, I've been so worried about you all. How are they?"

Sara smiled wearily at her partner. "Thanks for hanging around. Mum's just dropped off to sleep, she's exhausted. She has a few cuts and bruises. They're waiting for a bed to become available on the women's ward with the intention of keeping her in overnight."

"That's great news. And your father?"

Sara's gaze drifted to the other people seated in the waiting area. "I have no idea yet. He had a heart attack which caused the accident."

"Damn. What's going on with him?"

"He's being transferred to ICU where they'll monitor him. He's been under the specialist for a while for his ticker..." Suddenly everything overwhelmed her, and her legs gave way.

Carla caught her and led her to a spare chair in the corner. "Take it easy. I know this is a huge shock for you. You're going to have to remain strong, Sara. Your mum is going to be counting on you."

Sara covered her head with her hands and rocked back and forth in the chair. "I know. Fuck, Carla, I can't lose him, not now. It's too soon for him to leave us. Mum will never cope without him, they're inseparable."

"Don't think that way. I'm sure your dad will pull through this. If he's anything like you, then his determination will pull him through. Don't give up on him, try and think positively."

"I'm trying, believe me. It's hard, though. The last few years have taken a toll on me, and what happened with Mark a few weeks ago has left me more jaded than I thought possible. I might seem as if I've got my shit together on the outside, but inside, well, I feel like tiny fragments are being chipped away each time something like this happens."

Carla flung an arm around her shoulder and hugged her. "That's to be expected. We all get times when it feels like we have the weight of the world on our shoulders. You've had a tough few years to contend with, no one is doubting that, but please, don't give up now, not when your parents need you the most."

Sara sobbed. It was unlike her to break down, but it was the release she needed to move forward. Carla rubbed her back until her sobs subsided.

"Better?"

Sara turned to face her. "Better. I'm sorry. Things just got on top of me."

"No need to apologise. Want me to get you a coffee?"

"I should get back to Mum. I only popped out here to give you an update and to tell you to go back to work."

"Are you sure? I don't mind sticking around to give you moral support."

"No, I'll be fine. I'm going to ring Mark, let him know what's happened. I'm sure he'll come as soon as he's free."

"Ring him now. I'd rather not leave you in the lurch if there's a problem at his end."

"I need to compose myself first. Maybe a coffee would help." She grinned as Carla rolled her eyes.

"I'll sort that now." Carla left her seat and trotted over to the vending machine in the corner. She returned and handed Sara a cup of steaming hot coffee.

"Thanks, not sure what I'd do without you."

"You'd cope."

"Go on, you go, I'll be fine," Sara insisted, blowing on her drink to cool it down.

"Not until you've rung Mark."

Sara withdrew her mobile from her pocket and punched in a number that went directly to Mark's mobile. He sounded out of breath when he answered.

"Sorry, have I disturbed you?"

"Yes and no, it's not what you think. I was feeding one of the rats I have in for castration when he jumped out of the cage. I've been chasing the damn thing around the surgery for the past fifteen minutes. Anyway, enough about my absurd antics, how are you? It's unusual for you to call me during the day. Anything wrong?"

"I'm at the hospital."

"*What*? Why?"

"Mum and Dad had a car accident. Mum's okay, but Dad is in a sorry state."

"Meaning what?"

"He's had a heart attack, Mark."

"Jesus! Okay, give me thirty minutes. I'll wrap things up here and come down there. Are you at County Hospital?"

"Yes. The A&E department. Thanks, Mark. Carla is with me now, so please don't rush. There's nothing you can do for them, so take your time."

"Nonsense. I'll be there as quick as I can. I love you, Sara. Everything is going to be okay, I promise."

"I hope so," she replied, her voice catching in her throat as the emotion surged through her again. She dropped the phone into her lap.

Carla leaned over and hit the End Call button. "I'm glad he's coming. I'll wait until he gets here and then leave."

"I'll be fine, you go. Do me a favour when you get back to the station. Let DCI Price know."

"Of course I will. If you're sure you'll be okay?"

"I will. Go, shoo…and, Carla, thanks for coming with me, it means a lot."

They shared a hug, and then Carla left the reception area. Sara watched her until she turned the corner out of sight. She stared into her coffee cup for a few minutes and then had a word with the receptionist, letting her know that Mark was on his way.

"Don't worry. I'll bring him through as soon as he arrives."

"Thank you." Sara made her way back to where her mother was

sleeping and sat beside her, listening to her breathe, watching her chest rise and fall naturally. She couldn't help wondering how erratic her father's breathing was at that moment. She had to force herself not to think about him.

Her phone rang. Distracted, she answered it without checking who was calling.

"Darling, how are you?"

Sara rolled her eyes. It was Charlotte, her former mother-in-law. "Hi, I can't talk right now, Charlotte."

"What? Of course you can, just for a second. Can you come to dinner this weekend? I have a surprise for you."

Sara left the cubicle. "No, sorry. I can't."

"May I ask why?"

Sara couldn't help herself—she sighed heavily. "Because I have a life of my own to lead and can't drop everything to visit you when you ring up, Charlotte. This has to stop. Stop badgering me. I'm nothing to do with you now...now that Philip is no longer with us. I lead a very busy life. My weekends off are precious to me. The last thing I want to do is feel obligated to come and see you every time you summon me. It might surprise you to learn that the world doesn't revolve around you."

"Well, I never…" Charlotte hung up.

Sara kicked herself for snapping and telling the woman some home truths that had been on the tip of her tongue for months. Seconds later, a text tinkled. She read it and tipped her head against the wall she was leaning on. It was from Donald, admonishing her for being a bitch towards his mother. She sent a text back:

I'm at the hospital with my father. He's suffered a heart attack. No idea if he's going to pull through or not, so forgive me for speaking out of turn to your mother.

Shit! Sorry to hear that, Sara. Pass on our best wishes to your mother. I'll explain the situation to Mum. Keep us informed.

If I get the chance.

HAVING SENT HER REPLY, Sara shoved the phone in her pocket. She returned to sit alongside her mother, trying her hardest to block out the persistent Charlotte.

Mark appeared at the curtain around thirty minutes later. She left her chair quietly, careful not to wake her mother, and kissed him. She held back the emotion trying to emerge.

"How are you holding up?" he asked, kissing her forehead and then her cheek.

"I'm fine. Mum's fine, she's still sleeping, it must be the meds they've given her. No news on Dad as yet, though. That's the toughest part, the not knowing."

"I know, hang in there. If they're still assessing him, that could take some time, especially if he's unconscious and unable to tell them what's wrong."

"I know. I appreciate you coming. Sorry to be a pest."

"You're not, and it's my pleasure. I'm glad you rang me, I would have been disappointed if you hadn't."

Her mother stirred. "Sara, is that the doctor, dear?"

She drew back the curtain to reveal Mark. "No, Mum, it's Mark. He's come to see how you're doing."

"That's nice. Don't be shy, Mark. Come closer, let me see the man who has stolen my daughter's heart."

Sara's cheeks heated, and she held out a hand to Mark, encouraging him to say hello to her mother properly.

"Hello, Mrs Beaumont. Lovely to meet you. Sorry it's under such awful conditions. How are you doing?"

"Now don't go making me feel older than I am. You can call me Elizabeth."

Mark smiled and moved around the other side of the bed. He bent to kiss her cheek and clasped her mother's hand to his chest. "The pleasure is all mine. Now, what have you been up to?"

"It's that daft husband of mine. He took an interest in a tree and wanted a closer inspection, except he forgot he was driving the damn car at the time."

The three of them laughed. Sara stopped immediately realising the severity of the situation. Her father was gravely ill, and here she was laughing as if none of them had a care in the world.

They made small talk for the next twenty minutes or so and then fell silent when the doctor reappeared. "Right, we're going to be moving you up onto the ward soon, Mrs Beaumont. How are you feeling?"

"A lot better, Doctor, thank you. I'd rather go home if it's all the same."

"Nonsense. That's more than I dare do at this stage. Let's see how you go overnight and make plans to send you home tomorrow. You'll need looking after, though." The doctor turned to Sara.

"She'll be thoroughly spoilt, I promise you, Doctor." She made a note to ring the DCI to ask for a few days off. No one could blame her, could they?

"Good. Let's get you shifted then." He drew back the curtain, and a porter appeared.

Sara and Mark stood to one side to give them access to the cubicle.

Sara seized the opportunity to ask the doctor, "How's my father doing?"

"It's still early days now. We moved him up to ICU a few minutes ago. Once your mother is settled, you should be able to visit your father."

"Thanks, we will. Any change in his condition, Doctor?"

"None either way. We need to take that as a positive for now."

The porter wheeled her mother away. "We'll see you up there, Mum."

Her mother waved and rested her head back against the pillow during her journey.

"What's the prognosis, Doctor? I'm Sara's boyfriend."

"I really can't say any more than I've told Sara already. We're dealing with a waiting game. His body suffered from the impact, as you can imagine. There is plenty of healing that needs to be done before we can go any further with his treatment. He'll be in safe hands in ICU, that'll be the best place for him. Now, if you'll excuse me, we have another emergency en route that I need to prepare for."

"Thank you for the update, Doctor, and for caring for my father."

"That's what we're here for. Remain positive."

"We will."

Mark wrapped his arms around Sara.

She placed a hand on his chest. "I have a feeling Dad isn't going to make it."

He pushed her gently away from him. "That's nonsense. The doctor told you to remain positive, Sara."

"I know what he said. Sorry, I shouldn't have said anything. Let's go up and see if Mum's settled, then I want to visit my father."

He held her hand, and they hopped on the lift that took them up two levels to the women's ward. Her mother was eagerly awaiting their arrival. The nurse was fussing over her, and she was looking past her, staring at the doorway. Sara waved, and they both approached the bed.

"This is my daughter and her handsome boyfriend," her mother stated proudly.

"Pleased to meet you both. Your mother will be well cared for during her stay," the redheaded nurse said with a toothy smile.

"Thank you. Are you tired, Mum?"

"Do I look tired?" her mother asked, barely able to keep her eyes open.

"Yes. Why don't you have a snooze, and we'll be right back."

"Where are you going?" She sounded panicked.

"Not far. I thought I'd go and see how Dad is."

Her mother flicked back the duvet. "I want to come."

The nurse was quick to react and tugged the quilt back again. "Oh no you don't. You have a head injury. No gallivanting around the hospital for you, young lady."

"But my husband, he needs me."

"Listen to the nurse, Mum. We won't be long." She turned and left her mother's bed before she had the chance to argue further. "She's always hated hospitals."

Mark chuckled. "I really don't know anyone who jumps for joy at the prospect of being confined to a hospital bed, sweetheart."

"Smart arse." She blew out a breath. "I need to steady my nerves. It's horrible having a sense of doom draping itself around your shoulders."

"I'll place my arm there instead." Mark pulled her close, and together they sought out ICU.

She felt slightly better knowing that he was there with her. She doubted she'd be able to make this journey alone otherwise.

They reached ICU and peered through the glass panel in the door. It wasn't long before Sara spotted her father lying in the bed, his eyes firmly shut with three nurses fussing around him, fiddling with the equipment by his side.

She gasped. "My God, he looks terrible."

Mark hugged her. "He's just had a heart attack, love. It'll take a while for his body to recover from that. Keep positive."

"I'm trying. Gosh, I wish I could take his pain on board. I'm stronger than he is."

"I wish I could help out there, too. Maybe the scientists will invent something that will do that in the future. Now there's a thought... Maybe I should have a word with a few of my geeky friends who I went to college with."

She dug him in the ribs. "Good idea. We'll discuss it later."

A nurse glanced over her shoulder and gestured for them to enter the room. She rubbed her hands together and pointed down with her finger.

"Here, she's telling us to use the antibacterial gel." Mark stepped to the side a few paces and squirted a few blobs of the gel into the palm of their hands.

"Thanks."

Once they'd worked it in, they pushed through the door and approached her father cautiously.

Two of the younger nurses smiled and made their way back to their station.

The older nurse encouraged them to come closer. "Hello, I'm Sister Jeffries. I'll be in charge of your father's welfare while he's on the ward. I take it the doctor has spoken to you, made you aware of his situation?"

"Yes. He told us that they can't operate until he regains consciousness."

"That's right. His vital signs are a little off at present. That's understandable, given the trauma he's been through. We'll keep a close eye on him during the day and report back to the doctor regularly. Hopefully, we'll see an improvement in his status soon. Please, try not to worry. He truly is in the best place possible for him. I hear your mother has been admitted, too. How is she?"

"She's doing better than Dad. They're keeping her in overnight as a precaution. She'll be eager to see Dad when she can. They're inseparable, you see."

"We can arrange that. I could get a porter to go and fetch her and bring her up for a quick visit if you think it'll settle her down."

"That would be fantastic, thank you."

"I'll arrange that now, while you're here. It'll be more reassuring for her to have you here as well during her visit. I'm speaking from experience, of course. While I do that, why don't you talk to your father?"

Sara cringed. "Really? What should I say?"

The sister laid a hand on her arm. "Just be natural, talk to him as if he were awake."

"Okay, I'll try."

Mark reached for her hand and squeezed it. "You'll be fine."

The sister walked away.

Sara took a few tentative steps closer to the bed and leaned over to kiss her father on the cheek. She whispered in his ear, "Hello, Dad, it's me. I've brought Mark to see you. You're going to love him as much as I do."

Mark shuffled forward. "Hello, Mr Beaumont, it's an absolute pleasure to meet you. Sara talks nonstop about you and her mother. I can't wait to have a good natter about what Sara got up to when she was growing up. I'm sure she was a little devil."

Sara playfully swiped his arm. She was glad she'd decided to ring Mark. For a moment she had hesitated, debating whether to or not, her logic wayward at the time. He was part of her life and part of the family now, there was no reason to keep this type of thing from him.

Another ten minutes of chatter slipped past. Something squeaked —the door opening—and Sara's mother was being wheeled towards the bed, tears running down her cheeks.

Sara held her hand out to her. "He's fine, Mum. It looks scary, but he's not in any pain."

"Oh my, all that machinery. Is that keeping him alive?"

Mark coughed to clear his throat. "It's not as bad as it seems, Mrs Beaumont. Most of this will be precautionary because he's still unconscious. The second he regains consciousness and is able to tell the nurses what's going on, then most of this will be taken away." He glanced over at Sara.

She nodded her appreciation of his words. "See, that's a professional telling you how it is."

Her mother frowned, her gaze still fixed on her husband. "Didn't you say he was a vet?"

Sara chuckled. "He is, Mum, and a very good one at that."

"Okay. I'll take your word for that. How long before he comes around, any idea?"

Sara shook her head. "The body has to heal, Mum. That's going to take a little time. We're going to have to be patient until that happens."

"I suppose we have to be thankful he's still here." Her mother entwined her fingers with her husband's.

"Think optimistically, Mum. He wouldn't want it any other way."

Her mother nodded. They remained there, silently comforting each other for the next fifteen minutes or so.

The sister came across to them and said, "Why don't you all try and get some rest now. Mr Beaumont will be fine with us."

"If you're sure? I think Mum needs to get back to bed," Sara replied.

"I can speak for myself, Sara. Okay, I'm ready to go. Stephen, I'll be back to visit you soon. I need you to recover from this. I couldn't go on without you winding me up all day long." Her mother sobbed.

Fresh tears ran down Sara's cheeks, and she hugged her mother tightly. "Don't say that, Mum. We must think positively."

Sara stood upright and rolled her eyes at the sister.

She smiled at Sara in return and patted her arm. "He'll be fine. Let's get him through the next few days, and I'm sure he'll be discharged in no time at all."

"Really? That would be wonderful," Sara responded, standing behind her mother's wheelchair, ready to push her off the ward and back to her bed.

Mark dislodged Sara's hands. "I'll do that."

"Sorry, I'm so used to doing things myself."

"Not anymore, young lady."

She pecked him on the cheek, and the three of them left the ward. Her mother was quiet on the journey back, they all were.

Sara tucked her mother back into bed. "We're going to leave and let you get some rest now, Mum. I'll be back tomorrow to pick you up."

Her mother's eyes were drooping heavily. She settled herself down in the bed and fell asleep instantly. Sara and Mark left her to sleep and stopped at the nurses' station on the way out. She slid one of her business cards towards them and asked them to contact her anytime day or night if her mother wanted her.

They left the hospital, and Mark drove her back to the station to collect her car, then she followed him home.

"What do you fancy for dinner?" he asked, waiting by the front door.

"I don't think I could eat much. Don't let me stop you from eating, though, not that I have much in."

"Takeaway it is then. Indian or Chinese?"

"You choose. Don't get me anything, I'll nibble at yours."

He tutted and wagged a finger. "You need to keep your strength up for what lies ahead of you, Sara."

"I know. Okay, I'll have a korma. No rice, though. Get a naan, and I'll have some of that."

"Your wish is my command. I'll give them a ring now."

CHAPTER 9

HE WAS SEETHING, watching the news on the small TV screen in his dump of a bedsit. He hated this place. He hated everything. His life, what it had become since... There were days when he hoped he wouldn't wake up in the morning. It would solve a lot of his problems if he didn't.

His focus returned to the female newscaster telling the viewing public about the two fires which had happened, merely roads from each other within a few days. A smirk pulled his lips apart as he relived the details of each of the events. They deserved to die, for the way they treated me.

That's right, they did. The others will pay, too.

All in good time, all in good time.

He shook his head. The voices were getting worse. Driving him to do things that sometimes he consciously didn't know he was doing until it was too late. He shook his head again, trying to extricate the angry tones still wittering on in his head.

He opened the photo album sitting on the cluttered table in front of the flea-infested couch he was perched on the edge of. Her beautiful face lit up every damn page.

Kill her!

Yes, kill her. She's a bitch, and her life needs to end for what she's done to you.

Then he decided to leave the confines of his room and go for a drive. Still the voices persisted.

You know who should be next?

No, who?

That bitch and the kid. The one responsible for him living in a shithole!

She'll get her chance to push up the daisies.

A maniacal laughter filled his head. He shook it, but the laughter persisted. His temper rose. He planted his foot down heavily on the accelerator, and the car surged forward.

"Stop it. Leave me alone." He slammed on the brakes, aware that bringing attention to himself could be his downfall. He smacked his forehead against the steering wheel, hoping to chase away the voices plaguing him.

With the voices now silent, he started the engine again and drove to an address that had once been on autopilot for him.

He parked slightly up the road, the house visible from where he sat, the bay window at the front acting as a beacon for him to fix his gaze on. He'd loved that house and the people within it. It still flummoxed him as to what went wrong to change things, but something had destroyed his once happy life, driving it into the depths of depravity. Now it was the evil thoughts that guided his every move. His days were spent inventing ways to exact his revenge. The voices insisted he should hurt her, but he couldn't bring himself to do that. So, he did the next best thing: set out to hurt the people she loved the most. Those nearest and dearest to her, who'd been regulars in her life, in *their* lives. They would all be punished come the end, every last one of them.

He had to do it. To silence the voices. They drove his every waking moment. Forced him to think and believe evil thoughts that he never knew existed. He was under their spell. How long for, he didn't know.

He shifted forward in his seat when she glanced out of the window. Luckily, the car was shielded by a white van. He'd angled his own vehicle so he could peer out of the side window without her identifying it. His heart beat faster. Her beauty had always taken his breath away. She picked up the child, their child, and held her in her arms. They were waving at someone. He craned his neck to see who the person was, a jealous tic tapping at his right eye.

A man. He was walking up the steps to the house. Both the woman and the child were waving frantically at him. The man let himself into the house with his own key. *What the fuck? How? Who the heck is he? How dare he have a key to my home! How dare he!*

Fascinated, he craned his neck farther, stretching out the muscles until they became taut to the point of snapping. The man appeared behind the woman. He wrapped his arms around the woman and the child. The child wriggled, a huge grin on her face. The woman placed the child on the floor and fell into the man's arms. They shared a long kiss until the child forced them apart. The man and the woman laughed. The stranger swooped and picked up the child; she was laughing. His heart hurt, pounded the side of his ribcage. Tears moistened his eyes.

He hated the thought of this man being in his house. Sitting at his table, feet up on his couch, and worse still, sleeping in his bed next to his wife. *He* should be there, *not* this man.

Yet another one to add to the list.

We'll make him rue the day he ever laid eyes on the bitch.

"Stop it. She's beautiful. I won't allow you to think badly of her. I still love her. Still want her and my child in my life."

Then you know what has to be done, don't you?

Yes, do it, do it. DO IT!

His head connected with the steering wheel several more times. Blood trickled past his eye, and he swiped it away.

The man could wait. He had plans he needed to carry out first. He needed to stick to the schedule. He wanted to achieve the maximum impact on her heart, although, by the looks of things, maybe he was barking up the wrong tree. Maybe it was this man he should be targeting next. She didn't seem too upset by the other deaths. Did she know about them? She had to, it was all over the news now.

He bedded down for the night, his gaze never leaving the house. A hand squeezed his heart when all the lights went out downstairs and the light in the main bedroom went on. The man drew the curtains, the light still visible along the edge of the material, the material they had chosen together from Laura Ashley. They'd been the most expensive pair of curtains he'd ever forked out for because she had pleaded with him to have them. He'd worked overtime that week to ensure he paid for them without getting into debt. That all seemed a lifetime ago. That job as well as his marriage was a thing of the past. But his determination was such that he wanted his wife back in his bed and his child sitting on his shoulders like she used to.

He had no form of contact with either of them, she'd seen to that. He'd show her how much he'd changed, to get back in her good books. He'd lashed out at her a few times before their marriage had ended. He regretted that more than anything in his life. He'd lost his job at the factory—production was down, and they were forced to lay people off. He'd been one of the first to be handed his notice.

She'd been sympathetic but told him not to dwell on things and to get his butt out there and search for another job. He'd snapped. Struck her across the face. Their daughter had been in the room and screamed uncontrollably for what seemed like hours.

He'd left the house. Gone to the pub to lick his wounds. Not long after that the voices had started. With no job to go to, his life spiralled out of control within a few weeks. He lazed around the house, drinking cans of lager, not showing a bit of interest in either his wife or his daughter. Every time she nagged him, ordered him to get a grip, he backhanded her, regretting his actions soon after, even though the damage had been done. She'd finally had enough and called the police. They'd got involved and ordered him to leave the house. A restraining order was issued to keep him away from their child. It was still in place.

He was riddled with regrets for his behaviour. He'd tried to call her numerous times. She'd hung up in the beginning—that was before she'd changed the number. He'd kept his distance for months now. They probably thought he was either dead or had left the area, as he'd told her he was thinking of doing.

But a plan had quickly formulated in his confused mind and now he was acting out that plan. Damaging people's lives beyond repair, all because of *her*. Because she had dug her heels in to obstruct him taking part in their lives. He missed them. Missed the companionship they'd once had. The sex they'd had that had produced their beautiful, angelic daughter. Now, now, it was obvious she had moved on with her life. Forgotten all about him. Knowing that would drive him to punish even more people. He'd already added another name to his list this evening; he would make sure he added a few more for good measure. She would pay for robbing him of his once happy life. She would pay.

She'll pay.

Yes, she will. So will he.

HE WOKE the following morning at the first glimpse of the sun rising over the rooftops in front of him. He stretched out the kinks in his spine. He was getting too old for this kind of shit. Sleeping in a car instead of his bed all night was wearing on his body and his mind.

The man left the house and drove off in his sporty Audi, never once glancing back at the house. That showed how much he cared for her. When *he'd* left the house, she'd waved him off every morning.

One final glimpse at the bedroom window, no movement there, then he followed the man, intrigued to see where he would go. Work or home for a change of clothes? Presuming he didn't have any of his possessions at the house. He wasn't quite sure if her lover was wearing the same attire as the day before or not. He followed him back to a detached house, one of these executive-type homes out at Credenhill, and waited for the man to reappear again.

Thirty minutes passed. The man left the house, his hair still damp from a likely morning shower. He jumped in his car and drove into town. The traffic was building around the city centre by this time. The man turned down one of the side streets and parked behind a terraced house. He watched him enter the building and noted the plaque on the wall. Her lover was a goddamn dentist which meant he was on a decent wage, unlike him. His anger for the man grew to a higher level. He slammed his foot on the accelerator, and his tyres squealed when he drove away. He drove back to his crummy bedsit and threw himself on his bed. He lay there, staring up at the ceiling for a few minutes, his blood boiling as his temper rose. He sought out the notebook and pen under his pillow and jotted down a few pages of notes, things he intended doing over the coming few days. Adding to his already bulging agenda. Then he replaced the notebook under his pillow and smiled as he waited for sleep to come. He had nothing else to do with his days except sleep.

CHAPTER 10

SARA WOKE UP EXHAUSTED, emotionally wrung out by what the last twenty-four hours had flung at her. When she'd returned home with Mark the previous evening, she'd spent almost two hours on the phone to her brother and sister, trying to reassure them that their parents were all right. It might have been true in her mother's case, but definitely not in her father's. She was worried sick about him but she really didn't want it to come across that way to her siblings.

Lesley had got to the hospital herself around eight that evening and sat with their mother until nine. She'd rung Sara once she was at home. Her sister's resolve had shattered into tiny pieces. There was very little Sara could say to ease her sister's mind regarding what was going on with their father. Lesley was beside herself and told Sara that she had arranged to take the next few days off work so she could be with their mother when she was released from hospital the following day. This piece of news came as a relief to Sara. It also meant that she could concentrate on finding the brutal killer blighting her life at present.

She promised to ring Lesley periodically during the day for regular updates on both of her parents. Before leaving for work, she rang ICU to see if there was any change in her father's condition. There wasn't.

She knew her parents' well-being would be at the forefront of her mind, but she was determined to remain at work to continue her hunt for the killer.

Her first stop when she arrived at the station would be the DCI's office, to make her aware of what personal trauma she was going through, just in case she needed to cover her back.

Mark had been a valuable support to her, leaving her thinking what the hell she would have done without him if the gang who had kidnapped him had carried out their threat to end his life. She shook the dreadful thought from her mind and continued on her journey into work.

Carla had not long arrived herself. They hugged each other briefly, and Sara filled her in on her parents' status as they ascended the stairs to the incident room.

"You go on ahead. See if anything new has happened overnight. I'll have a quick word with the chief."

She wandered along the narrow corridor and walked into the DCI's outer office. Mary glanced up at her and then cast her eyes down at the diary beside her.

Pre-empting what the secretary was about to say, she shrugged. "Sorry, I need to see the chief on a personal matter. Is she free?"

"She is. Let me ask her if she has time to see you."

Mary left her desk, tapped on the chief's door and walked into the room. She opened the door and beckoned Sara a few seconds later. Sara squeezed past Mary and nodded her thanks before Mary closed the door behind her.

The chief set her paperwork aside and gestured for Sara to join her. "Personal matter? What's this about, Sara? Carla mentioned your parents were in hospital."

She flopped into the chair opposite the DCI and clenched her hands together in her lap. "That's right. Mum should be discharged today—my sister is going to take care of her—but Dad is in ICU. If I get a call, I'll need to dash over there at a moment's notice."

"Of course, that goes without saying. It was a car crash, wasn't it?" Carol Price's brow furrowed in concern.

"Yep. Mum's just got a few cuts and bruises. Her stay in hospital was precautionary, but Dad suffered a heart attack."

"Oh, my Lord! Why are you here? Don't answer that, you're amazing; however, in this instance, you should be with your family."

"I disagree. My sister is holding the fort with my folks. I'm not worried about Mum. Dad is a different story. Although there's nothing I can do for him. He's in ICU; they'll ring me if there's any change. Please, I need to be here. To keep myself occupied. It'll do me no good being at the hospital, thinking only negative things about my father's condition."

The DCI shook her head. "I don't agree with you, but the decision is yours. Is your team aware?"

"Yes, don't worry, they won't let me down. Carla will be with me every step of the way today, ensuring I don't slip up. We need to catch the bastard who is causing havoc on our patch, and soon, before he escalates."

"I trust you. If, however, you feel things are getting on top of you, please, please tell me. Deal?"

Sara rose from her chair. "Thanks for understanding, boss. I won't let you down, I promise."

"I know you won't, you never have. Keep me informed about your parents."

"I will." Sara smiled and left the office.

She walked into the incident room a few minutes later. The team all turned her way when she entered. Sara knew that Carla had saved her the job of filling them in. "Right, as you're all aware, that's the end of dealing with my personal issues today. I'll just see what crappy paperwork awaits me and I'll be with you soon. A coffee would be most welcome if someone wants to take pity on me and buy me one," she added, trying her best to lighten the sombre atmosphere emanating in the room.

Several chairs scraped, but it was Barry who reached the vending machine first. Sara entered her office and groaned at the mail sitting on her desk. She paused at the window to admire the view for a few seconds. Barry placed the coffee on her desk then retreated.

"You're a treasure, thanks, Barry. Any updates that need my immediate attention?"

"Frustratingly no. Nothing to report as yet, boss."

"Okay. I'll be out in about half an hour by the looks of this lot," she said pointing at the mountain of brown envelopes lying on her desk. "We'll do some brainstorming then."

Barry nodded and left the room. Sara sat and began tackling the post. Half an hour later, she'd whizzed through it all and was ready to start the 'real police work' as she liked to refer to it.

She wandered over to the whiteboard, and the rest of the team angled their chairs to face her. "Okay, let's start from the beginning. Have we had the fire investigation report yet?"

"Not yet, we're still awaiting that," Carla replied.

"Make a note to chase it up when the meeting is over, Carla. I know these things take time, but bloody hell, we need to get this bastard caught, and quickly. Anything come to fruition from the house-to-house?"

"One of the neighbours at the second incident saw a black car driving past the scene that he didn't recognise. He's kicking himself that he didn't take down the registration number," Barry said.

"Okay, if I recall rightly, didn't Sylvia Trent, the neighbour at the first fire, say the same?"

Barry nodded. "She did. Want me to check the CCTVs around that area at the time?"

"You read my mind. If that's all we have to go on, then yes, thanks, Barry. Anything else? Any other calls come in following the airings on TV and radio?"

"Nope, a very disappointing response so far," Carla admitted, tapping her pen on her cheek.

"Yet another case that is perplexing us. We need a break, guys. Hopefully we'll obtain that when either the fire investigation team or the pathologist gets back to us. All we can do for now is keep digging into the victims' past, see what shows up there. So far, they've all been model members of the public." She dismissed the team and went back into her office. She was busy making a few notes when the phone rang. Fearing it was the hospital ringing, she answered it hesitantly. "Hello. DI Sara Ramsey. How may I help?"

Heavy breathing sounded down the line. *Oh crap, it's been a while since I've had one of these!*

"Hello, Inspector. Sorry, I thought I better give you a call. You told me to contact you at any hour of the day if I thought of something."

"Hello, sir. Who is this?"

"Blimey, you must think I'm a right idiot. It's Lawrence Swanley, you're dealing with my daughter and son-in-law's case."

"That's right. How are you, sir?"

"Bearing up. My wife can't stop crying, though. That's the toughest part, trying to console her. It's hard dealing with our grief, trying to figure out why someone would do such a horrendous thing."

"I can appreciate that, sir. My heart goes out to you." She was dealing with personal pain of her own, only hers was considerably less given that her mother and father were both still alive. "What can I do for you?"

"It's the other way around. Jane and I were sitting here last night watching the news when something clicked."

"Oh, what was that?"

"It was the first we'd heard about the other fire. The thing is, I believe my daughter was friends with the Webbs."

"What? They knew each other?" She kicked herself for not asking the couple when she was at their house.

"I want to be more definite about that, but I can't. Jane thought it would be best to ring you to let you know. Maybe you can delve into it further."

"Thank you for ringing me. Every snippet of information we can gather at this stage could be vital. We'll dig into it and see what we can find out. I really appreciate you calling me. Take care of yourself and your wife."

"You're welcome. If anything else comes to mind, I'll be sure to ring you."

"Thank you, that would be wonderful. Goodbye, Mr Swanley." Sara rushed out of her office and clapped at the doorway to gain everyone's attention. "I've just received a call from Kristina Swanley's father to say his daughter was friends with the Webbs."

"My God. Don't say I was right?" Carla muttered.

"About this having to do with the Neighbourhood Watch Scheme? It's plausible, Carla. It's another angle that we need to look into. How close were the families? Other than that, I'm still at a loss what to suggest."

Craig raised his hand as if he were back in school.

Sara grinned at him. "The toilet is down the hall on the right, love."

The young detective's cheeks coloured. "I was going to suggest that I go back out there and conduct further house-to-house enquiries now we've gleaned that, boss."

"Sorry for teasing you, Craig. I'd say you have a valid point. Who wants to volunteer to go with him?"

Will nodded. "I'll do it, boss."

"Thanks, Will. Can you go to both areas, see what you can find out? While you're gone, I'll ring the other relatives of the victims and tentatively ask if they're aware of a relationship between the two families." She went back into her office and sought out the contact information for Tina's mother, Cynthia, and rang her.

"Hello, Cynthia, this is DI Sara Ramsey, we met the other day."

"Yes, I remember. Please tell me you're ringing to say you have news about my family?"

"In a roundabout way, I suppose I am. I'm not sure if you're aware of another incident which happened close to Tina's house, perhaps you've seen it on the news?"

"No. I can't bring myself to watch the news right now. I suppose I've been guilty of wallowing in my grief since the fire."

"I'm sorry to hear that. It's come to my attention that Tina and Malcolm might have been friends with the victims in another fire that we're investigating. I wondered if you could confirm that and tell me what sort of relationship they had."

"Really? Who?"

"Kristina and Paul Stonehouse."

She sucked in a harsh breath. "My God, no! Yes, they were best friends. You're telling me they're dead as well?"

"Unfortunately, yes. Although their deaths were significantly different to your daughter's." Sara swallowed down the bile filling her mouth then continued, "The couple were murdered in their home just before their house was set on fire. A neighbour managed to see the fire before it really took hold and called the fire brigade. They put the fire out quickly, and that's when Kristina's and Paul's bodies were discovered."

"This is truly shocking. Murdered. I knew them. I've met them a few times at Tina's barbeques. My goodness, why on earth would anyone want to kill them? Why? None of this makes any bloody sense at all."

"I'm sorry if I've upset you further. I wondered if you could enlighten me as to what their relationship consisted of." The question sounded awkward even to Sara's ears, but it was aired now, and there was no going back.

"They were best friends. They have been for years. I've no idea when that friendship began, my mind is too fuzzy to think of that, sorry. They were so close that when a house came up in the area near to Tina, Kristina and Paul jumped at the chance to become neighbours. They were always in and out of each other's home when time permitted. Umm…hang on, yes, they were both godparents to Tallulah, Tina and Malcolm's daughter."

"Wow, they must have been really close then. Okay, thanks for the insight. We'll dig further, see what shows up on our radar. Was it just them? What I mean is, was it just the four of them, or were there other friends they were really close to?"

"A couple of others—please don't ask me to name them—my head is spinning as it is with what you've just told me. Maybe if you give me a chance to think about things, I can call you back either later today or tomorrow."

"Whatever suits you. It could be vitally important in the investigation. Sorry to heap things on you like this."

"Don't be. I'll do what I can to help the investigation. The information may take a while to surface in my muddled mind."

"I understand completely. Ring me when you can." Sara ended the call and sat back in her chair. The link was evident. Now all they had to do was find out why someone wanted the two families dead. Could it be that they had fallen out with one of the neighbours? Ganged up on someone to make them see sense about a neighbourhood issue? Or could it be work related? No, she didn't think that was possible because all the adults worked in different fields. This had to be something personal, but what? Everyone they had spoken to so far had reinforced that all the victims were kind people and that they couldn't understand why anyone would want to harm them.

She threw her pen across the desk, just missing Carla as she entered the room. "Sorry, that's my frustration showing. Anything?"

"Nope. I wondered if you wanted another coffee. What's up?"

"Turns out that Kristina and Paul Stonehouse were godparents to Tina and Malcolm Webb's daughter. So that means they were exceptionally close friends."

"Bugger. There's something fishy about this case, isn't there?"

"You're not wrong. It's back to the drawing board on this one."

CHAPTER 11

RAGE FILLED his every move as he got ready for his next venture. Dressed all in black, he jumped in his car and set off, his balaclava sitting on the seat beside him. He swore when he messed up the gear changes in his haste to get to his destination.

Tackling the traffic, he managed to get there with a few minutes to spare. He parked on the double yellow lines at the back of the building and waited, drumming his fingers on the steering wheel, darting his gaze around, surveying his environment, not only on the lookout for a job's worth traffic warden but also for nosy passers-by who could possibly identify him and his car.

A few women left the rear of the building. He turned his head in the other direction and waited for their giggling chatter to fade before he focused on the back door once more. His heart raced, and his stomach tied itself into knots, a blob of apprehension mixing with the rage that had drawn him to this location. No one else left the building after the women had departed. Taking a chance, he started the engine and let it idle for a few minutes, his gaze fixed on the back door.

Seconds later, his wife's lover flung open the door and headed for his car.

One final look around him and he drove his car a few feet, intentionally blocking in the man's car. He turned his head away from the man, in case he looked in his rear-view mirror, and placed the balaclava over his head.

The man jumped out of his vehicle and marched towards his car. He got out of his car and stared at the man who'd come to a juddering halt the second he saw the balaclava.

"What the fuck are you doing?" the man demanded, swallowing noisily after he asked the obvious question.

"You'll find out. Get in your car." He waved the knife, letting him know that he wasn't messing around.

"Why? Here, take my money. That is what this is all about, isn't it?" The man dug in his jacket pocket and produced his bulging wallet.

"Wrong. Get in the damn car, or I'll slice you into tiny pieces."

"Okay. I'm doing it now. Stay calm."

Those words...are you going to let him get away with that?

The voices had started. He wanted to scratch his head to erase them but decided to ignore them instead.

The man got behind the steering wheel of his Audi and sat there, his hands trembling, the colour swiftly draining from his face. "If it's not money you want or need, then what? Do I know you?"

"You probably know of me, and what you've been told I'm guessing wasn't complimentary. Why? Why are you with her?"

"Who?"

He thrust the knife towards the man's neck, the blade nicking his skin.

"Ouch! Please, don't hurt me. I don't know who you're talking about."

"Think again. Listen to the question properly next time. Why are you with *her*?"

The man gulped. "Who? Claire?"

"Hooray, the man has a brain after all. Yes, Claire, my wife."

His eyes widened. "What? She told me you were divorced."

"That's a trivial matter. We promised to love, honour and protect

116

each other for the rest of our lives. In the eyes of God, we're still a unit."

"Hey, man, I don't want any trouble. I'll walk away, she means nothing to me."

Was he openly admitting that he was using Claire? The despicable shithead. She was nothing more than a good lay in his eyes. How low could a man get? "And yet, you shared her bed last night. Are you telling me that meant nothing to you? The fact she probably gave herself freely in our bed...and it meant nothing?"

The man fell silent. He could tell he was scrambling to find the right words to reply.

"Man, look, if you want her back, then I promise I won't stand in your way."

"You'd walk away from her and my daughter with a click of your fingers as if their feelings meant nothing. Is that it?"

"No. That's not what I'm saying. Have them, if they mean that much to you. To be honest, I think she's still in love with you anyway."

He smiled beneath the balaclava. He knew she wouldn't be able to move on, not a hundred percent without him by her side. If there was a way back into her bed, he knew what he needed to do.

Fucking twat... Kill him.

Yes, the using bastard. He's the type to dump her and be in someone else's bed by nightfall. Kill him.

The voices were driving him nuts, blocking out the way he'd thought this was going to pan out. Now he was confused. He should strike, leave the man sitting in a pool of his own blood and get out of there. Maybe go back and try to sort things out with Claire. He was desperate to hold her and his daughter, Amelia.

He was torn. Did he kill him or could he trust the man to walk away as he had promised he would?

You're a thick shit if you believe him. Finish him off now. Go on, I dare you!

Yeah, do it. Do. It.

"Your type makes me sick. I bet you used your silver tongue to get into her bed, didn't you? Cheap words that meant fuck all. For what? To get inside her knickers. Do you ever think of the trauma you're causing? Playing with people's feelings like that? Have you told her you love her?"

The man stared at him in stunned silence. He could tell the man was unsure whether to admit he had or not.

He jabbed the knife under his chin. "The truth. How long had you been seeing her before you mentioned the L word?"

The man shuddered out an anxious breath. "Two weeks."

"Two frigging weeks. When did she open her heart up to you?"

"Around the same time. Please, don't hurt me. You can have her. I'll walk away."

He'd heard enough. He found it abhorrent how someone could mess with a woman's feelings like that. The knife slipped to the man's stomach. He stabbed him a number of times before the man realised what had happened to him and put up any form of struggle.

"Men like you make me want to vomit. The world will be a better place without you. Take that, you bastard. God may have given you handsome features on the outside, but inside you're ugly. Pure evil."

"No, please. Stop! Don't do this. Don't kill me."

Someone blasting their horn in the road behind them drew his attention back to the present. "You're lucky I don't have time to kill you. I promise you, I'll be back." He turned away from the man, removed his balaclava, tucked his knife under his black jumper then exited the car. "Sorry, mate. I'll be right there. Just having a natter with my buddy."

"I couldn't give a toss what you're doing. Move your damn car and stop blocking the road, moron."

His temper bubbled once again, but he decided to fix a smile in place and wave an apology at the driver, even though he was tempted to slice his throat. Thinking about it, he'd missed his opportunity. He should have done the same to Claire's new boyfriend. Now he'd have to drive around the block and come back to finish off the job. He hopped in his vehicle, and his wheels squealed when he drove off. The traffic was heavy in the rush hour, and it took him nearly ten minutes to return, only to find the man's car was missing.

"Shit! Where the fuck did he go?" He scanned the immediate area. Nothing, no sign of the Audi anywhere.

Now you've done it, fecking idiot!

Yes, you dickhead, you should have finished him off.

"Shut the fuck up. Leave me alone to think."

It's a pity you didn't think before, instead of letting the prick get away.

Dumbass piece of shit. No wonder Claire wanted rid of you.

He slammed on the brakes. The car behind him screeched to a halt and blasted its horn. He bashed both sides of his head, trying to rid himself of the voices. He'd had enough of them. They were driving him insane. Making him do things he didn't want to do. Wouldn't have dreamt of doing when he was with Claire. Where had it all gone wrong?

A horn blasted behind him again, reminding him that he was in the middle of town, caught up in the heaving traffic. He raised a hand to apologise to the driver ticking him off. Although, he was tempted to get out of the car and jab him with his kitchen knife.

"What the fuck do I do now?"

You can be a dumb shit at times. Go to Claire's house. That's where he'll be heading.

No, he'll be on his way to the hospital.

Listening to the voices confused him even more. In the end, he decided to drive past Claire's house to see if the Audi was parked up there. Fifteen minutes later, with his nerves tauter than a tightrope, he arrived at Claire's address. He searched up and down the road, no Audi in sight, but he spotted her looking out of the front window, obviously anxiously awaiting the man's arrival. Something she'd never done for him, not to his knowledge anyway. She'd pay for that, or if not her, someone she knew would.

He drove home to get changed, another dangerous mission lying ahead of him that evening. He left the house in the same sort of get-up he had worn on his previous adventure. He drove to the new location and reclined the seat a little. There, he could keep an eye on the house without being spotted. There was one car already in the drive, her car. It wasn't long before the second car arrived. The time was approaching eight o'clock; it would be getting dark soon. As soon as the darkness descended, he'd make his move.

Furious at himself for dozing off, he woke with a start and glanced at the clock on the dashboard. Eight-fifteen. He was late. He hated running late. It had always appeared unprofessional to him when he'd been working. The night was closing in around him now, giving him the shield he needed to make his next move. He approached the house, his black holdall by his side, the large kitchen knife in his hand, and rang the bell. He just had enough time to pull the balaclava in place before the man opened the front door.

The man appeared shocked. His first instinct was to try to slam the door shut in his face, but he was quick to realise what was about to happen and jammed his foot in the gap.

The man ran into the house, shouting, "Janice, Troy, run out the back, quickly."

"Do that and I'll kill him," he bellowed.

They ended up in the lounge, all three members of the family gathered together in a huddle. The first thing he noticed were the cards dotted around the room. Words of endearment for the engagement party that he'd been invited to and then uninvited just as quickly. So they'd gone ahead with it. "When's the big day, have you decided yet?"

The couple faced each other, confused.

The man spoke for both of them. "Next year. Please, what do you want? We don't have much money, we're in debt up to our eyeballs."

"Ha, and yet you're planning a big wedding. Why not trawl up to Gretna Green and be done with it? It'll only cost you a couple of hundred quid. You guys have been living together for years anyway, right?"

The couple glanced at each other again.

This time the woman spoke, "Do we know you?"

He laughed. "Yep. Can't you guess who I am?"

The couple shook their heads in unison while their child looked up at them.

"Mum, Dad, who is it?"

The woman placed a protective arm across the boy's chest. "I don't know, love."

"You do. What if I were to say that you invited me to the party and then rescinded the invitation? Ring a bell, does it?"

She gasped. "William, is that you?"

He laughed, throwing his head back. He didn't care that she knew who he was. She wouldn't be around long enough to tell anyone anyway. "Give her a pat on the back from me, Lucas."

"Why? What do you want from us, William?" Lucas asked.

They had been close drinking buddies at one time, until he'd lost his job, then the man had dropped him like a tonne weight. That had hurt him, an indescribable pain that no one deserved to endure.

He threw his bag on the floor in front of him and looked at their child, Troy. "Boy, open the bag and get the rope out."

"Please, I'm begging you to leave him out of this. Let him go," Janice pleaded.

"No can do. I need him to be my assistant, and then…well, you'll soon find out. Do it!" he shouted.

The boy shot across the floor, landed on his knees and tore open the bag. He gasped when his hand touched the objects inside.

"Only get the rope out for now," William instructed, amused by the fear causing the boy to break out in sweat.

The boy sank his hand back into the bag and extracted a length of tightly bound rope.

"Good, now undo it. Watch you don't tie it into knots. I've got a close eye on you. Don't mess up or waste time."

Troy glanced up at his father.

William bent down and got in the boy's face. "You listen to what *I* tell you. Don't go asking for permission from them. I'm in charge, got that?"

"Y…e…s," Troy stuttered.

With the length of rope untangled and laid out on the floor,

William ordered the parents to drop down. "Sit down. Troy, I want you to tie your parents' hands behind their backs. No funny business. If I think the rope is too loose, well...I'll..."

Troy nodded, his head bouncing up and down vigorously. "I get it. I'm a Boy Scout, I know how to tie a good knot."

"Good."

You chose well. He could be valuable to us in the future. It would be a shame to kill him.

I agree. Hang on to the little twerp, he's eager to please and liable to do anything you ask.

"Shut up," he muttered, fed up of listening to the voices.

The boy stared up at him. "Sorry?"

"Nothing. Go on, do as you're told. Be quick about it. Do you have a badge of honour for your knot tying?"

"Yes, I've got ten badges altogether. I'm a quick learner."

"Excellent. Show me what you can do, Troy."

He watched as the boy swiftly tied his parents' hands. His mother was talking to him, praising him and telling him how much she loved him. Reassuring him not to be scared. Janice had always been a good parent. He remembered that with such fondness that for a second, he doubted what he was doing. The family were nice, apart from the way they had treated him. If only people had been less disrespectful, he wouldn't have been driven to such lengths.

The house phone rang. Everyone fell silent.

"Ignore it. Don't even think of answering it, Troy."

The answerphone kicked in, and he found himself mesmerised as Claire's voice filled the room.

"Janice, are you there? I need to speak to you, something dreadful has happened. Have you seen the news? I don't want to mention it without speaking to you in person. Call me back immediately. I'm scared."

"What have you done, William?" Janice asked when the call ended.

He shrugged. "Nothing much. Anyway, you'll find out soon enough. I wouldn't want to spoil the surprise. Troy, be quick, son. On to your father now."

"Leave Troy out of what you have planned for us. You'll scar him for life," his father pleaded.

"You leave me to worry about that. Sit there and shut up. Take your punishment, you hear me?"

Lucas nodded, and his shoulders sagged in resignation.

His face was itchy. Now that the family had figured out who he was, he decided to remove the balaclava and slipped it into the bag.

Troy announced nervously, "All done. Do you want to check my work?" He sat back on his heels and pointed at the bindings he'd put in place.

William tugged at the ropes and nodded. "Excellent work. You deserved the badge you received, Troy. Now, take the knife from the bag."

"No, don't listen to him, Troy," his mother shrieked.

William stepped in front of her and slapped her around the face. Her head snapped to the right with force.

"Shut up! Don't interfere when I'm dishing out instructions, got that?"

"I'm sorry," she sobbed, bowing her head in shame, unable to wipe the blood pouring from her nose.

"The knife, Troy. Remember who's in charge here."

Troy grabbed the knife and held it awkwardly. "What shall I do with it?" he asked, his voice shaking.

"I'm going to tell you now. Have patience, son."

He shuffled behind the boy and sat on the floor, close to him. "I want you to take the knife and stab your father. If you don't, I'm going to slice your right ear off."

"I can't...I can't do that," Troy sniffled, clearly completely overwhelmed by the suggestion.

"Don't make him do that, William. You're not being fair on the lad," Lucas pleaded.

Troy hesitated. William grabbed his ear and wrestled the knife from his grasp.

"Don't take me for a fool, boy. This is your last chance. Now do it!"

Troy trembled from head to toe and held out his hand for the knife. William placed it in his hand at the same time his mother sobbed and his father shouted, "Do it, Troy. We love you, no matter what you do to us, we would never blame you."

William laughed, tipping his head back. "Yes, do as you're told, and I promise not to hurt you."

Troy was crying now, his tears mingling with the snot running from his nose. "Please, I don't want to hurt either of them. There must be another way out of this. Don't make me hurt my parents. I love them, they've been good to me. They're the best parents in the world."

William lowered his head and sneered at the boy. "They've given you their blessing, now do it. This is your final warning." He slapped Troy around the face, ensuring he got his point across.

"Don't hurt him," Janice shouted. "He'll do as he's told. Listen, Troy, we'll love you no matter what you do to us under duress. We understand you're in a tight spot. Do what you have to do to survive this."

William smiled tautly at her. "Glad to see you realise you're in a tough situation and there is only one way of getting out of it. Boy, this is your last chance, either you stab your father or you can say goodbye to your ear." He leaned in closer. "And that'll only be the first of the body parts you lose, you hear me?"

Troy closed his eyes, his mouth moving as if he was uttering a silent prayer. He plunged the knife into his father's stomach. It hit his belt buckle, and Troy glanced at William in fear.

Seething, he glared at the boy. "You know what to do."

Sighing a juddering breath, Troy plunged the knife a second time, this time much higher than his first attempt. He sobbed when his father cried out in pain.

William applauded the kid's bravery. "Well done, young man. I'm sure your parents are very proud of you. Now...do the same to your mother." He grinned at the terrified eleven-year-old.

Troy shook his head. "Please..." he whined. "I can't do it. Don't make me. I'll do anything else but I can't hurt my mother."

"That's a shame. Wrong answer. You're gonna have to suffer the consequences of refusing that order."

He snatched the knife from Troy's hand and swiftly sliced off the boy's ear before he had time to realise what was happening. Troy's screams mixed with his mother's. William covered the boy's mouth with his hand. Troy tried to detach himself from William's grasp, but he held him tight.

"I'm warning you all to be quiet or I'll be forced to use the other implements I have in my bag."

Troy stared at his mother, blood gushing from his wound. "Forgive me, Mum."

Janice swallowed and nodded. "Do what you have to do to save yourself, son."

Troy squeezed his eyes tightly shut and angled the knife towards his mother's stomach and pressed it through her clothing.

She cried out in pain but whispered over and over, "I love you, son. None of this is your fault. God won't blame you when it comes to Judgement Day."

William laughed again. "If there is one. Do you really believe that if there was a god he would allow evil people like me to exist in this world? That the likes of ISIS and the Taliban would still reign supreme in certain areas, beheading innocent people with their swords?"

Janice was a devout Christian. They'd had this same conversation over the years at social gatherings they'd attended together.

"Don't listen to him, Troy. Stick with your beliefs and what we've instilled in you over the years. God won't desert you; he'll never do that. He's watching you now, seeing that you're carrying out these despicable deeds under duress. Stay strong, my lovely. Stay strong and live a happy life when your father and I are gone. Nanna Paula will take care of you. She'll ensure you grow into a man we'd be proud of walking the streets. Live life to the fullest. Don't let this blip affect your future. Be thankful in the knowledge that your father and I are leaving this world together. We'll make the journey to Heaven hand in hand with no regrets. We're so proud of you. You're our greatest achievement in this world, don't ever forget that."

"I'm sorry, Mum. Please...don't...leave me..."

Janice's eyelids drooped. She tried to keep the smile in place for her son's sake, but William could tell she was losing consciousness quickly.

He issued a final insult: he applauded her speech and smiled as her eyes closed. Her last vision on this earth would be of William grinning at her.

Troy broke down in tears, his own injury long forgotten. His tears were for his parents.

"Troy, listen to me, son. You'll go on from strength to strength once this man lets you go. Go to Grandma Paula's house. She'll raise you as her own, with love and compassion. Your mother and I are so proud to have known you, to have raised you. We've never had any regrets, and neither should you going forward. We love you..." Lucas's voice trailed off. The red splodge on his white shirt spread rapidly, and his eyes struggled to stay open during his speech.

William was smug with retribution coursing through his veins. No misgivings whatsoever for putting this loving family through such evil transgressions. His own happy family unit had been destroyed the day he'd lost his job. It wasn't fair on him to see others happy when his life was so damn miserable. They'd messed with his head, included him in what should have been a wonderful celebration, and then snatched it away as though they could no longer trust him being around them. This was a satisfying conclusion for him. Once Claire realised what was going on, she'd think twice about the way she had treated him, throwing him out of the house and divorcing him within a few months before he'd managed to get his head around his new life.

He snapped out of his reverie and stared at the boy. He patted him on the back. "You did well. You should be proud of yourself, son."

Troy stared at him, his eyes wide at his words as if trying to fathom what William was on about.

"This isn't over with yet. Go to the bag and fetch the hammer."

Troy's gaze shifted between his dying parents, the bag and William.

"Be quick about it," he shouted, drawing his hand back, ready to slap the boy again.

Troy scrambled across the floor on his hands and knees and returned with a heavy claw hammer. William noticed a change in the boy's eyes and anticipated his next move. Troy lunged at William, the hammer held high above his head.

William grasped the boy's forearm. "I wouldn't if I were you."

"I hate you. I've always hated you, you're a weirdo. I told all my friends that you were weird..."

"Oh, did you now? Okay then, let's really see what you're made of, young man. I want you to strike your father's head."

Troy released the hammer from his shaking hand. "No. No more. He's dying, let him die in peace now."

"He's not but he will be soon. Either you strike your father, or I tie you up beside them and leave you to die with your parents. What's it to be?"

You're not going to let him get away with that, are you?

You've got no balls. If you had, you'd come down heavy on the lad.

"Shut up," he warned the voices, seething that they were forcing him to punish Troy. Hadn't he gone through enough already?

"What?" Troy asked, frowning.

Punish him. The lad isn't going to do what you say.

Yes, strike him. The vile creature has no right to disregard you. Do it. Punish him.

He went over and over the words in his head. The voices were right. Troy was disobeying him. Time was getting on, and he needed to get this over with quickly now. He snatched the hammer from the boy's hand and smashed it into first Lucas's head and then Janice's. Troy screamed. William withdrew an oily rag from his pocket and shoved it in the boy's mouth, silencing him. Then he returned to his holdall and removed a length of rope. He crossed the floor towards the boy and yanked his arm, forcing Troy to drop to the floor and sit next to his parents, then he wound the rope around the three of them. Troy sobbed and gagged on the rag, and his eyes flew open in sheer panic.

"Hush now. The more you fight, the worse it will become. I know I said I wouldn't hurt you, but you attempted to hurt me. You shouldn't have done that, sonny."

Are they dead? The parents?

Go on, check their pulses. You must make sure they're dead before you kill the lad. He has to know that they're dead.

Doing as the voices instructed, he checked first the father's pulse at his neck and then the mother's. Nothing. They'd both taken their final breath in this world.

"Are they still alive?" Troy asked, the words just decipherable through the rag.

"Nope, they're dead. Don't worry, you'll be joining them soon." He laughed. The boy's petrified face was a picture. The air suddenly smelt of urine.

"Have you wet yourself?"

"I'm sorry. Please, I'm scared. If you let me go, I promise I won't tell anyone what happened. It'll be our little secret." Again, his words came out muffled but distinguishable.

"Nope, I can't trust you. You tried to hurt me. That was a foolish move."

Troy coughed, and the rag moved in his mouth as the boy's tongue tried to dislodge it. The rag fell out, but William did nothing to replace it.

"I was confused. I didn't know what to do for the best. Please, don't punish me for that. We could become a team, you and me. What do you say?"

"It's a matter of trust, lad. You tried to strike me. That was your biggest mistake today."

Troy's chin dropped onto his chest. "I'm sorry. I regret that now."

"Trying to achieve self-preservation will be your downfall at the end of the day." He went in search of his bag and removed the petrol canister from it. He circled the family, emptying the contents of the can, chuckling as he watched the liquid soak into the deep pile of the fawn carpet.

The boy sobbed and muttered a prayer, something about delivering his soul along with his parents', from what William could hear.

He didn't care. Christians had their way of worshipping that didn't sit well with him. It never had. Yes, he'd got married in church, but didn't everyone? What did it truly matter? His anger was building up inside again. He needed to get out of there quickly. He finally looked in the boy's direction, and their gazes met. He felt nothing, no remorse for what he was about to do. As far as he was concerned, his life was over anyway. It really didn't matter how many other lives he snuffed out in the process.

He gathered his bag, dipped his hand inside to retrieve the lighter and held it to the liquid pooling closest to the door, ensuring that he wasn't cutting off his own escape route. The flames spread quickly, the boy's screams following him out of the house. He ran down the path and tripped over a dog as he rushed out of the gate. The dog growled, and the owner holding the leash appeared livid that his pet had been hurt. *For fuck's sake, what is it with folks walking their dogs in this area?*

"Oi, watch where you're going. You hurt my dog. He's not happy now."

"Screw your damn dog, and screw you, old man." He raced across the road to his car, flung his bag into the back seat, and yanked open the driver's door. He started the engine and glanced back at the man with the German Shepherd.

What the fuck are you doing? He's a witness, he needs to be silenced.

Yeah, idiot. Go back and stick your knife in him and that damn dog.

William shook his head. Flames engulfed the lounge in the house behind the man. No, as much as he knew the voices were right, he realised he needed to get out of there, sharpish. He pressed down hard on the accelerator and flew past the man who was shaking his fist at him. William peered into his rear-view mirror, shock registering on the man's face when he twisted to see the flames over his shoulder. The man took out his phone, and that was the last William saw before he turned the corner at the end of the road.

Fecking arsehole! He's gonna dob you in now.

Yeah, he's probably got your licence number as well.

You really are a prime knobhead.

Maybe you should do a runner, escape while you can.

The voices taunting him stoked his anger. He wished they would do one, leave him be, but there was no fear of them doing that in the near future. Not until his agenda had been fulfilled.

* * *

"Emergency, which service do you require?"

"Please, get me the police and the fire brigade. There's a house on fire in Chelmsford Drive. Hurry. I can hear someone screaming inside."

"Okay, sir. They've been dispatched. What's your name, sir?"

"Mike Post. Please, tell them to hurry. I saw a man leaving the house. He did this. I didn't know it at the time. I saw him. I can identify him."

"That's brilliant, sir. A patrol car will be with you shortly. Will you remain at the scene until they show up?"

"Of course I will. I want them to catch this bastard. Oh God, I had no idea he'd caused the fire. I thought he was just in a hurry when he left the house. He came hurtling out and tripped over my dog. I wish Rex had bitten the arsehole. Excuse my language. Oh great, I can hear the sirens in the distance. Thank God for that. Shall I hang up now?"

"Yes, thank you for taking the trouble to ring us, sir. They'll be with you shortly, they're a few streets away now."

"Goodbye." Mike ended the call and paced the pavement across the road from the house. He'd moved farther away in case the windows blew out or something. He had to protect Rex. The dog was his only companion since his wife had died of cancer eighteen months before. Tears misted his eyes as her face drifted into his mind, and he tried to push the image aside but found it impossible. His thoughts were also with the poor people trapped inside the house. He knew Janice and Lucas, they were lovely neighbours, always tucking his bin away for him when he forgot about it. They also kept an eye on his property if he went away for the week to Dorothy, his daughter down in Brighton.

A police car screeched to a halt beside him, and the fire engine also arrived seconds after.

"Mr Post?" the young ginger-haired officer asked.

"That's right. You did well to get here so quickly. Please, you have to help the family. I heard screams a while back, nothing since then. It sounded like the child. Janice and Lucas have a son around ten or eleven, a quiet lad, never any bother. Do you think this was an accident? What am I thinking…? No, it must have been that damn man. He must have set the fire before he rushed out of the house. Oh heck, I'm waffling. I'll shut up now."

The officer stroked his upper arm. "Don't worry. We'll get the fire put out ASAP. So, you're telling me you saw the man? Can you give me a description?"

"I could pick him out in a line-up. Not sure I could give you an accurate description while my mind is on that damn fire. That poor family, please, you have to help them."

The constable pointed to the firemen pulling out their hoses. "It's all in hand. They'll be in there tackling it in a moment, sir. Did you see where the man went?"

"He drove off in his car. A black Renault, one of the older type models, no idea which one exactly."

"That's good enough, sir. I don't suppose you happened to notice his registration number?"

"I did. PEJ 280Y. Gosh, I've shocked myself there. I'm usually hopeless at remembering details like that."

"Excellent news. Let me get on to the control centre with that information." The constable walked away a few paces, placed the call and returned. "Let's hope we can find that vehicle soon. Did you recognise the man, sir?"

He thought over the question with a niggling feeling gnawing at his gut. "Actually, I think I do know him. Not by name, only recognised his face, now that you've mentioned it."

"Interesting. Do you think he's a regular visitor around these parts or do you think he lives around here?"

"I think the former. I didn't recognise him that well, not like I would if he were a neighbour. Oh my, I've just had a thought... You don't suppose this is connected to the other fires that have happened in the neighbourhood recently?"

The young constable shrugged. "Possibly, sir. Excuse me while I place another call."

CHAPTER 12

THE PHONE RANG and Sara cringed. Her brother's bloodshot eyes narrowed when he glanced her way.

"Sorry, I have to take this." She walked out of her mother's lounge and into the hallway with her brother's words ringing in her ears.

"No, you don't, but you're going to anyway."

She closed the door and answered the call.

"Hello, ma'am. Sorry to disturb your evening. I thought you might want to hear about this ASAP. There's been another fire within a few streets of the others."

She sighed and then let out a low growl. "Okay, it's not the best time for this to descend on me, but I'll attend. Give me the address, Sergeant."

The desk sergeant gave her the address which she jotted down in her notebook, then she ended the call and returned to the lounge, prepared for an onslaught from her brother's sharp tongue.

"Sorry, I've got to go. There's been another incident in the case I'm working on."

"You're kidding me," Timothy snarled.

"Pack it in, Tim. If Sara has to go, it's got to be for a good reason.

Mum's settled anyway, and we'll both sit here with her for a while. Sara, you go," Lesley insisted with a genuine smile.

Sara pecked her sister on the cheek. "Thanks for understanding, Lesley." She bent down and hugged her mother gently and kissed her on the forehead. "Glad to have you home, Mum. I'll check in on you tomorrow."

Her mother waved her hand feebly, still a little weak since her return home. "You've got a murderer to find, dear. All I ask is that you keep me up to date with what the hospital says about your father."

"I'll ring them every few hours and let you know if there is any change, Mum. Take care. I'll drop in tomorrow. It'll probably end up being a late one tonight, given the circumstances."

"Your brother and sister will keep me company. You just concentrate on finding your suspect, dear. Thank you for coming."

Sara smiled at her mother and her sister who was also accepting of her situation. Her brother followed her out of the room to the front door.

"How could you, Sara?" he slurred.

She shook her head. "There's no point trying to explain what I do to you, Tim, you probably wouldn't understand."

"Oh, I understand all right. You're a workaholic, you always have been. Putting that damn job of yours first before your family."

Sara's blood boiled. She closed her eyes as she slipped on her coat. *Not again! He is always condemning me for being the ultimate professional. This was nothing different. It just stung more, knowing that her mother had just been discharged from hospital and her father was still fighting for his life.* She lowered her voice and glared at him. "Don't do this, Tim. Not now. I neither have the time nor the inclination to point out how wrong you are. What harm would it be for you to stay here with Mum, looking after her for the next day or so? Let's be fair, it's not as if you have a family of your own to attend to, is it?"

She winced, and he flinched as her own damning words filled the air between them.

"I suppose you're going to tell me that you think it's my fault I'm no longer married and I have been forbidden to see my kids until I clean up my act."

"I'm sorry. I really didn't mean that. You always come down heavy on me for being a police officer. Why can't you just be proud of the work I do?"

He fell silent.

"I don't have time for this bullshit now. I'm sorry we still don't see eye to eye on my role in society, Tim. I've got to go. Take care of Mum for me."

"I will. It's my duty to do that as her only son."

The way he'd said it was as harsh as if he'd battered her over the head with a baseball bat.

"I'll check in later. Try and hold off drowning your sorrows until then."

She slammed the front door as she left, regretting her final dig as she ran towards her car.

As much as she tried to prevent it from happening, the conversation repeated itself several times in her head during the course of her journey. She was tired, tired of constantly fighting with her alcoholic brother whose life had imploded since his wife had taken their two kids and walked out on him. She didn't know where they were now— Tim made sure no one knew. She'd never figured out why that was. She'd tried numerous times to speak to him calmly about the subject, but they'd always ended up rowing about it. It was her parents she felt sorry for. They were missing out on seeing their only grandchildren grow up, which in the end, put pressure on Sara and Lesley.

Lesley was in the process of planning her summer wedding to Brendan. Hopefully, once they tied the knot, they'd lighten the load on that score, and her sister would fall pregnant straight away. It wasn't as if Lesley didn't want kids, unlike Sara. Her brother was right in that regard—she was devoted to her work to the detriment of having a life of her own. Maybe that would all change in the future, now that Mark was a constant feature in her life.

Sara arrived at the scene thirty minutes after she'd received the call. She hadn't bothered ringing Carla—her partner would probably give her earache for that, but there was method in her madness. She needed Carla to be on top of the game during the normal working day, in case Sara slipped up at all.

"What have we got?" she asked the young constable who had walked away from a gentleman with a German Shepherd.

"Sorry for getting you out, ma'am. I rang the station, and the desk sergeant twigged that this might be connected to the cases you're already working on."

"It's no problem. Have the brigade put the fire out?"

He glanced back at the house in question. "Yes, they're packing up their things now, ma'am. The person in charge is over there." He pointed to an older man in uniform.

"Okay, I'll have a quick word. The man you were talking to, who's he? A nosy neighbour?"

"Definitely not, ma'am. The perpetrator bumped into him when he left the house. He's been really helpful, given me the reg number of the Renault the man was driving."

"Wow, have you circulated the details?"

"Of course, ma'am. The witness, Mr Post, also said he recognised the man as being a visitor around here."

"Excellent news. Can you get a statement down for me?"

"Of course. I'll do that now."

Sara smiled and crossed the road to speak to the fireman in charge. She flashed her warrant card and introduced herself.

"Can I get in there?"

"I'd leave it a few minutes. SOCO are on their way. One of my guys went in there and found three bodies in the lounge. Not a pretty sight. Looks like they'd been tied up. He said a couple of the victims—the two adults—appeared to have open wounds to their heads."

Sara frowned. "Wounds that occurred before the fire was started perhaps?"

"SOCO will have to be the ones to tell you that. We need to get tidied up; there's nothing more we can do here now."

"Thanks for attending and putting the fire out so promptly."

"If you've got an arsonist on your hands, I hope you find the bastard soon, for all our sakes."

Sara let out an exasperated sigh. "So do I." She walked a few feet away and stared at the front of the house for a few moments and then dug out her mobile. She called the desk sergeant.

"Hi, Jeff, it's Sara Ramsey. One of the constables at the scene told me he had a possible reg number for the perp. Have you circulated the details?"

"I did that immediately the information came my way, ma'am. I put out an urgent appeal. I've heard nothing positive as yet."

"That's a shame. We need to stop the vehicle, and soon. Ensure everyone is aware how dangerous the driver is."

"I'll do that, ma'am. Anything else?"

"Nope, just keep your eye on the ball for me, Jeff. I sense we're closing in on this fucker."

"I'll let you know as soon as anything comes my way."

"Brilliant." After ending the call, Sara approached the house and peered through the front window. There was a gap at the side of the curtains that gave her a glimpse of the horrendous scene that awaited her and the SOCO team when they arrived.

Turning away, she surveyed the road. The firemen were in the final throes of storing their equipment, and two patrol cars were on the scene. Four constables had set up a cordon around the house and were shepherding the crowd of neighbours back. Sara made her way over to the witness who the constable was taking a statement from. She introduced herself.

"Carry on, Constable. Think of me as an observer only at this point."

The constable nodded and asked Mr Post another question. "So, when he came out of the house, can you tell me if he was carrying anything, sir?"

"Yes, he had a black holdall in his hand. He was dressed all in black. Had he not tripped over Rex, I probably wouldn't have noticed him as the light was already fading when the incident occurred."

Sara smiled at the witness. "I want to thank you for calling nine-nine-nine right away."

"My pleasure. I take it the family didn't survive?"

She shook her head. "They didn't. We'll know more about what happened when SOCO arrive."

As if saying that summoned them, a SOCO van, a motorbike and an ambulance arrived within seconds of each other. The rider of the motorbike slipped off the helmet to reveal shocking red hair.

"Goodness, who's that?" Mr Post enquired, his mouth dropping open slightly.

"That's the pathologist."

"Oh my. Slightly different to what I was expecting after watching *Quincy* all those years ago."

Sara chuckled. "I'll tell her you said that, sir. If you'll excuse me."

"No, don't. I didn't mean to cause offence."

"You haven't. She's used to people thinking she's different, I promise you." Sara crossed the road to the newcomers at the scene. "Unusual for you to turn up on your bike, Lorraine. You're causing quite a stir among the natives."

"I know, sorry. I was on my way home when the call came in. I decided to come straight here, knowing how anxious you'd be to get answers."

"A bit presumptuous of you to think I would be the attending officer."

"I was right though." Lorraine grinned. "Anyway, I don't have to be Einstein to work out the three incidents are connected."

"I know, dreadful, isn't it? We've got a lead, though. The gentleman over there saw the perp leaving the property, clocked his vehicle." She held up her crossed fingers. "Only a matter of time now, I'm guessing. Can I enter the house with you?"

"Fantastic news. It's about time you caught a break on this one."

"I'll say."

Sara walked alongside Lorraine to the SOCO van. Lorraine had a brief word with her forensic team and handed Sara a white paper suit, gloves and blue covers for her boots.

A few minutes later, they were both standing in the living room of the house, surveying the gruesome scene.

Sara swallowed hard, trying to hold down the bile clawing at her throat. "Shit! What type of person does this to a family?"

"A fucking arsehole with an evil agenda would be my guess off the top of my head. Of course, that's a personal opinion and not a professional one."

"I'm inclined to agree with you. Sick shit. The fucking world is full of them at the moment."

"An age-old problem, I think you'll find, Inspector. Which I believe goes back centuries to when law enforcement didn't exist."

"Let's not go there. Deaths in the dark ages were horrendous betrayals to humanity as far as I can remember from history lessons at school. Looking at this scene, the killer knew what he was doing. Looks like he battered the parents over the head with something. The question is, did the boy see his parents die before the fire consumed him?"

"Time will tell on that one. What is definite is that these poor people suffered during their ordeal. The fire was a deliberate act; they were tied up. There's evidence of that, and my take is that petrol was likely poured around them. They had no chance of escaping the flames whatsoever. You're dealing with a twisted SOB as my American counterparts would say."

"Sickening." Sara cast her gaze around the room and noticed something blinking on the sideboard under the window. She pressed the button on the answerphone. A woman's voice tumbled out of the machine, her tone urgent, fearful almost.

"What are you thinking?" Lorraine asked, startling her when she appeared by Sara's side.

"I'm thinking I need to try and trace the caller. Sounds like she knows something."

Lorraine nodded. "I agree. You do that, and I'll help my guys assess the scene."

Sara left the house, leaving Lorraine to instruct her team on what she wanted from them. "Hi, Jeff, yes, sorry, it's me again. Will you do me a favour?"

"Shoot, ma'am. My pen is ready and waiting."

"Good. I've found a call on the family's answerphone. I need to trace where that call came from."

"I'll get on it right away, ma'am. It might take me a few hours to get an answer for you."

"Do your best and let me know, no matter what time the results come in. I'm going to finish up here and head home. I'll be in earlier than usual in the morning, so I might see you before you finish your shift."

"I'll see what I can do for you."

Sara ended the call and returned to the lounge. Lorraine's colleague was photographing the crime scene from different angles. Once he'd finished, Lorraine inspected the three victims with Sara close by, looking over her shoulder, asking a question now and again.

"Okay, to me this injury to the man's head seems like he suffered a blow from a hammer to me."

"Can you tell me if that injury occurred post or pre-mortem?"

"I'd say after he died. The perp was ensuring the man was dead." Lorraine knelt on the floor next to the female victim. "Yep, as I thought, this injury is very similar, same depth and width to the hole in the man's skull."

"Gruesome. Why wasn't the boy struck in the same way?"

"No idea. I doubt we'll ever find that out either. Studying the boy carefully, he appears to have dried blood on his face. My guess, he suffered a possible nosebleed. Nope, hang on, his right ear has been chopped off."

"Shit, wicked fucker! So, he had to watch his parents' lives end and was still alive when the fire started. Not sure which is worse—dumb statement, of course, I know. That poor lad. Why? Why would someone feel the need to put a child of...ten or eleven, at a guess, through that?"

Lorraine heaved out a sigh. "He must have had a reason. Bloody hell, he must be warped to do that to the kid. The poor thing must have gone through hell, watching his parents die, knowing he wouldn't be far behind them."

Sara closed her eyes and remembered reading the witness statement. "Damn, the witness said he heard the boy screaming."

"Aww, man, that fucking hurts!"

"You're telling me." Sara wiped a stray tear away with her forefinger.

"Okay, look, there's nothing else for you to do here. Let me deal with the family now. I'll get the PM reports to you within the next few days. Why don't you go home?"

"I think I will. It's been a traumatic few days personally for me."

"Oh, why? I hope your fella is all right and hasn't had any fallout from his ordeal up in Liverpool?"

"No, Mark is fine. It's Mum and Dad. They were involved in a bad accident. Dad suffered a heart attack and smashed into a tree. He's in a coma in ICU, and Mum was discharged today."

"Shit, Sara. I had no idea. Why the fuck are you still working?"

Sara tilted her head. "You really want me to answer that?"

"No, don't bother. I'm sure I'd be the same as you if I were in your shoes and knew there was an odious killer on the prowl."

"We're two of a kind in that respect, Lorraine. You might be weird-looking but you have a genuine heart of gold, someone who cares about people they've never met."

Lorraine smiled. "You've nailed it. Except the part about me being weird-looking. You're lucky I like you and regard you as a soul sister, otherwise I might deck you for saying that."

Sara laughed. They both stood, and Sara hugged Lorraine, harder than she'd intended by the way her dear friend yelped.

"Sod off home, Sara. You've done your bit by showing up here. No one can doubt your commitment after putting in a full day's work."

"Thanks, love. Speak to you soon."

Sara disrobed at the front door and placed her protective clothing in the black bag that had been anchored down by a pot of spring flowers on one side of the door.

Wearily, she drove home, noting the time was almost ten on the

141

dashboard clock. "Damn, it's too late to check on Mum." Instead, she rang the hospital en route.

The ward sister informed her that her father's condition hadn't changed since she'd rung that morning. She told the sister she'd ring back in the morning and hung up.

She wasn't really one for saying prayers, not since she was a kid at school where she'd been forced to attend church, going to a Church of England school. Nonetheless, she offered up a small prayer for her father's quick recovery during her journey.

Mark must have been looking out for her. He opened the front door to greet her after she'd parked on the drive. She kissed him and then made her way into the kitchen.

"I'm beat. I need a coffee and I'm peckish. Fancy a piece of toast?"

"I'll do it. You sit down." He guided her to the table.

"Thanks. It's been a tough night. I rang the hospital on the way home. No change."

"I rang earlier myself."

"That was kind of you, thanks, Mark. My brother had a go at me earlier for running out on Mum to attend the crime scene."

"Don't be too harsh on him. He's worried about your mum and probably doesn't understand your commitment to your job."

"Unlike you." She smiled.

The kettle had finished boiling, and the toast popped up. He slathered the butter on and placed milk and sugar in the mugs then deposited them on the kitchen table. "I do my best. Sometimes it's hard getting a handle on what you go through. If people really thought about how coppers worked, they'd appreciate the emotional turmoil you put yourselves through in your quest to bring criminals to justice."

Taking a chunk out of her slice of toast, she placed her free hand on top of his. "Some cases cause us more 'emotional turmoil' than others, though."

He smiled and stared down at his mug. "I'm still trapped sometimes." He poked the side of his head. "Sometimes I'm back there, being tortured by those thugs. It was hard, Sara, damn hard. I dread to think how long it would have taken them to end my life if you hadn't been such an astute officer."

"Mark, you need to get past this, for your sake. Please consider seeing a counsellor?"

"I will. I didn't mean to let my self-pity show its ugly head, not when you're concerned about your parents. What I was trying to say in a clumsy way, is that I get it. I understand what you put yourself through in your role as a copper. It takes a special kind of person to deal with some of the worst criminals walking this earth, and you're up there with the best of them. I love you, Sara Ramsey."

She had trouble swallowing the mouthful of toast because of the lump that had formed in her throat. She took a sip of her coffee to try to shift it. "You're amazing, too. If you hadn't saved Misty a few months ago...well, I'd probably still be sitting here in tears now, grieving for her as well as for Philip."

He shrugged. "It's all in a day's work. Being a vet is nothing compared to what you do day in, day out."

"I appreciate that, Mark. I beg to differ, though. Drink up. I have to be back at work first thing, so I need to go to bed. This case just got even tougher. I won't bore you with the gruesome details."

"Thanks, I can do without hearing about them." He picked up her plate and ran it under the tap.

Then the pair of them took their mugs with them and went upstairs to bed.

CHAPTER 13

Sara had only managed to catch a few hours when she received a phone call from the station. "Hello, who is it?"

"Sorry, ma'am, it's Jeff. You told me to ring you once I found out who made the call to the latest victims."

Sara sat up in bed and switched on the light.

Mark threw the quilt over his head beside her.

"Okay, I'm ready. What have you got, Jeff?"

He supplied her with a name, phone number and an address.

"That's fantastic. I'll contact the woman when I get into work in the morning."

"Sorry to have woken you, ma'am."

"Nonsense. I told you to. Goodnight, Jeff."

She ended the call, switched off the light and snuggled into Mark.

"Not sure I'll ever get used to being woken up in the middle of the night. Rarely happens in my job, except for emergency cases," he grumbled, his voice muffled by the quilt.

"I know. I'm so sorry. It was important, though. It means I can tackle it as soon as I get into work instead of wasting half the day waiting for the information to turn up."

"I know. I just think it could have waited. It's not like you're going to do anything with the information now, is it?"

"Point taken. Sorry, Mark."

He mumbled a 'no need' and fell silent. Sara's mind whirred like an extractor fan for the next half an hour until sleep finally descended.

The alarm woke them at six. Sara jumped out of bed and into the shower while Mark went back to sleep. She dressed and dried her hair in the spare bedroom and placed a gentle kiss on the top of his head before she flew downstairs and saw to Misty's needs. She didn't bother boiling the kettle. Instead, she left the house within half an hour of her alarm going off.

Jeff was just finishing his shift when she arrived. "Long time on duty for you, Jeff."

"Short staffed as usual, ma'am. I've got a day off now, not that I have anything planned except sleep."

"Enjoy. See you soon."

She entered the building and ran up the stairs. The vending machine was her first port of call before she ventured into her office. She let out a relieved sigh when she spotted only a few envelopes sitting on her desk, vying for her attention. Sara dealt with them quickly while she waited for the rest of her team to arrive. At eight, voices drifted in from the incident room.

She called out, "Who's that?"

Carla poked her head around the door. "Me and Barry. Crikey, how long have you been here?"

"A while. Let me know when the team is all here. There's been a development overnight that I need to bring to everyone's attention, then we need to pay a visit to someone first thing."

"Sounds ominous. Are you going to tell me who?"

"In a while. Let me deal with this dross first and I'll reveal all."

"I'll give you a shout when we're all in. The others shouldn't be long. Need another coffee?"

"Always. Thanks."

Carla returned with a welcome cup of coffee and then left her to it.

It wasn't long before Carla returned to tell her that the team had arrived. Sara finished her coffee, almost scalding her mouth in the process, and joined the rest of them.

Sara filled in the details on the whiteboard as she spoke. "While you were all tucked up in your beds last night—actually it was way prior to that, knowing what time most of you get to bed. Anyway, I digress. I received a call to attend yet another fire. I arrived at the address to find the fire brigade had successfully put out the fire at the residence, but when I entered the house with Lorraine, we found the family sitting up in the middle of the room on the floor. They had been tied up, even though their bindings had been burnt and draped around them. The parents were probably dead before the fire started. However, they had a son, maybe ten or eleven, who was still alive when the house was torched. How do I know? Because a witness who called nine-nine-nine heard the boy's screams." She paused to let that nugget of information sink in.

The team all murmured their disbelief and disgust.

"Yes, yes. I feel the same way, of course. The thing is, we need to crack on with this. The perpetrator actually bumped into the witness as he was rushing out of the house."

"That's excellent news, isn't it? He'll be able to ID the person in that case...unless he was wearing a disguise or a mask, right?" Carla suggested.

"He wasn't, and yes, the man can ID him in a line-up. The witness also informed me he recognised the man as a visitor to the neighbour-hood, although he couldn't share a name with me. He was a tad shocked by what he'd witnessed and after he heard that the three members of the family had died in the blaze. When he rang nine-nine-nine, he informed the control room of the perp's car details, including the reg number. We need to chase that up this morning. Christine, I need you to do that for me."

"Will do, boss. You need the person's name and address, I take it?"

"Exactly. Let's track this bastard down today if possible. Carla and I will be visiting someone else soon..."

"Who's that?" Carla interrupted swiftly.

"While I was in the house, I noticed the answerphone was flashing.

A woman had rung the family to ask if they'd seen the news. My guess is this woman knows something relating to these crimes. What that is at present I have no idea." She glanced up at the clock on the wall. "Almost eight-thirty, a reasonable hour to start phoning people, I believe. I'll ring her now, see if she's up to seeing us this morning. I need the rest of you to crack on with the usual, see if there are any links to the previous victims. I have a hunch there will be. Barry, once Christine has the car details, I want you to register it with an ANPR interest."

"On it, boss."

"Good. I have a hopeful feeling running through me this morning, team, don't let me down." She went back into her office to make the call. "Hello, is this Claire Mawdesley?"

"It is. Who wants to know?"

"I'm DI Sara Ramsey. Would it be convenient if I popped round to see you today?"

"I suppose so. What's this concerning?"

The woman sounded a bit offhand to Sara. "Nothing that you need to feel worried about. We'd just like you to help us with our enquiries into a case we're dealing with."

"What type of case?"

"Please, any further details I'd rather say face to face."

"Very well. I have to take my daughter to playschool in a moment. I should be home by around ten past nine. Is that convenient for you?"

"The earlier the better. Look forward to seeing you then." Sara hung up and sat on the edge of her desk, glancing out at the view she'd come to love, her mind racing, wondering what she was about to learn from this woman. She returned to her seat and jotted down some notes just in case she forgot what questions to ask in the interim, what with her mind still elsewhere, concerned about her parents. Then she rang ICU. The response from the nurse was the same as before. Her father had a comfortable night as far as they could tell.

There was a knock on the door. She looked up to see a grinning Christine standing in the opening.

Sara gestured for her to enter. "Well? What have you found out?"

Christine glanced down at the sheet of paper she was holding. "The car belongs to a William Mawdesley."

She reeled off the address, but Sara was already aware of what that was. "You're kidding me? Bugger, this throws a different light on things."

"How so, ma'am?" Christine's smile slipped.

"Carla and I are going to visit Claire Mawdesley in less than half an hour. She rang the latest victims and left a message on their answerphone. Shit, what if she was ringing them to try and warn them about William?" She replayed the message in her mind on a loop. No, she didn't get that impression at all. "Ignore that. Her message wasn't a frantic one, not in that sense." She held her head in her hands and shook it.

"Want me to do the background checks on the couple, see if I can get those started before you set off?"

"That would be fantastic. Tell Carla to be ready to go in twenty minutes. Do your best to find me something before we go."

"I will. Leave it with me." Christine rushed out of the office.

Sara leaned back in her chair, her mind galloping with the facts that were unfolding at breakneck speed now, or so it seemed. Maybe this case could be wrapped up within a few days if they managed to locate Mawdesley and his vehicle, or was that wishful thinking on her part?

Shrugging on her jacket, she picked up her car keys and headed out of the office. "Anything, Christine?"

"Something to get you started. The couple recently got divorced, in the last few months anyway."

Sara nodded. "Okay, that's altered the direction of things for the second time this morning. Carla, are you ready? We'll be in touch once we've spoken to Claire. Keep up the good work, guys."

Running down the stairs with Carla behind her, Sara got a rush from the adrenaline pumping through her veins.

"Hold on, where's the damn fire?" Carla asked breathlessly when they reached the car.

"That's a bad choice of words in the circumstances, but I'll let you off. Anyway, sweetheart, I can't help it if you're unfit. Maybe I should have a word with that hunky fireman of yours, tell him he's not giving you enough of a workout in bed."

Carla's mouth dropped open and then slammed shut again, and her cheeks reddened. "There's no need for you to do that. Oh bugger, why do I bite when you wind me up?"

Sara laughed and jumped in the car. "It's so easy."

THEY DREW up outside the semi-detached home which had a number of steps leading up to the front door. A woman was peering out of the impressive bay window and waved when she saw them.

She opened the door and welcomed them with an anxious smile. "Come in. I'm Claire."

They flashed their IDs, and Sara introduced herself and Carla. Claire smiled and led them into the large lounge that was dressed like a show home, with a collection of throws and cushions adorning two vast, gold-coloured fabric sofas. Either side of the sofas was a small side table, an elegant lamp standing on each of them, the bottom of which was made of glass. The shade was a mid-grey tone that complemented the gold sofas.

"Please, take a seat. What is it you wish to speak to me about?" Claire asked.

Sara and Carla both sat on one of the sofas while Claire sat on the other. "First of all, I'd like to ask if you know a Janice Baxter."

"Yes, she's one of my best friends. Why?"

"When was the last time you contacted her?"

"Yesterday. No, that's wrong. I tried to speak with her, but she didn't pick up, so I had to leave a message on the answerphone instead. I presumed she was either busy or out."

"What time was that?"

"Around seven."

"May I ask why you were ringing her?" Sara's heart pounded hard.

"I wanted to share some bad news with her, ask her if she'd heard about our other friends. They lost their lives this week. I had no idea until I heard it mentioned on the news."

"Really? What are your friends' names?"

"Tina and Malcolm Webb, and Kristina and Paul Stonehouse." She ran a hand through her short brown hair, tucking a few strands behind her right ear.

"My team and I have been investigating the cases this past week. I'm sorry to have to tell you that yesterday, around the time your phone call was received, Janice and her family died in a fire."

"What? No, this can't be happening. Not again." She jumped out of her seat, paced the room for a few moments, and then dropped onto the sofa again. She grabbed a cushion to hold in front of her and rocked back and forth as tears rolled down her face.

"I'm sorry. There was no easy way of telling you that."

"Why? Do you know why?"

"We don't know the motive right now. Claire, maybe you can tell me where your ex-husband is?"

"William? I don't know and I don't care. Why do you want to know?" She gasped as if realising what was going on. "You don't think he's responsible for this? That can't be right. He wouldn't do this. *Never.*"

"Do you have an address for him? We searched the database, and his car is still registered to this address. Have you seen him lately?"

"I thought he was staying with friends. He didn't give me the address. I told him to keep this address on things until he felt he was settled somewhere. He seemed pleased about that, almost as if it was a weight off his mind."

"Why did you get divorced?"

"It was my fault. I fell out of love with him a few years ago and finally plucked up the courage to tell him. I read all these stories in the magazines how women stick with a loveless marriage but, to be honest, I didn't want to become a statistic. He wasn't happy about it at first, thought he could possibly change my mind. Even started buying me flowers and leaving little gifts around the house. Most women would find that appealing. I'm afraid I didn't. All it did was give me the creeps. I saw how he watched other men when we were out, the way they touched their partners. He tried to do the same to me but, come the end, I couldn't stand to be in the same room as him. I know that makes me come across as a wicked person and, if it does, then I'm sorry."

"Not wicked at all. If your love for him ended a while ago, then your feelings towards him were totally reasonable. Sorry, you didn't answer my question: have you seen him lately?"

She let out a long-suffering sigh. "No, I have a restraining order against him."

Sara's interest piqued. "May I ask why?"

"Because of his odd behaviour towards Amelia when he took her out a few times. One day, she came back in a very confused state. When I questioned her about what her father had said or done, she told me he kept asking questions about me and what I'd been up to."

"I see. Did he suspect you were seeing other men?"

"Yes. I wasn't, not at the time."

"But you are now?"

Claire bowed her head and placed the heel of her hand against her forehead.

"Claire?"

"Yes, at least I was."

Sara and Carla glanced at each other and frowned.

"Can you tell us what you mean by that?" Sara prompted.

"Gareth has been a regular visitor to my home for the past few months, virtually moved in a couple of weeks ago. He didn't come home last night."

"Has he rung you?"

"No. I tried ringing his mobile and all I seem to get is his voice-mail. I've left dozens of messages. Now I'm thinking that he no longer wants to know me and has given me the boot."

"Have the pair of you argued?"

"No. Gareth isn't like that. Actually, that's why I fell for him. He's a very loving man, treats me and Amelia with respect. He and William are polar opposites. William used to beat me senseless. I didn't want to say that before in case I came across as the bitter ex-wife. Gareth has never raised his voice to me, let alone his fist."

"And when did you last see Gareth?"

"Yesterday morning. He left here and went straight to work."

"Have you tried ringing his workplace?"

"Yes, they said they haven't seen him either. This is totally unlike him. I'm so upset by what has gone on this week. What with the fires..."

"We're sorry about your friends. Something came to light at yesterday's incident."

She dropped her hand from her face and glanced towards the window, tears welling up, threatening to fall. "What's that?" she asked, looking as if her thoughts lay elsewhere now.

"We have a witness who said that your former husband left Janice's house just before the fire started."

Her head swivelled quickly, and her eyes widened. "What? You think he did this?"

Sara shrugged. "It's definitely something that we're going to look into, which is why we need an address for him. As I said before, all our system is giving us is that this is his address when it clearly isn't now."

The dam broke, and Claire covered her face as the tears and the sobs began.

"Can you make some tea, Carla?" Her partner placed her notebook and pen on the coffee table and left the room.

Sara left her seat and perched on the arm of the sofa next to Claire. She slung an arm around her shoulder, and Claire turned her head against Sara's jacket.

"Let it out, Claire. It's been a traumatic time for you. I'm sorry about your friends."

Suddenly, she tugged away from Sara and plucked a tissue from the box sitting on the coffee table. "You don't think...?"

"What, Claire?" Sara replied, her brow furrowing, unsure what she was getting at.

"Gareth? You don't think William has got to him, do you?"

The thought hadn't crossed Sara's mind, but yes, from what Claire had just told her, that was now a very clear possibility. "I really don't know. We won't know that until we find William. Please, can you think of where he might be? Was there a special place the pair of you used to visit? What about his parents? Do they live in the area?"

"No. They're up in Scotland. I can give you their details, but he wasn't that close to them, not really. So I doubt very much if he would go there."

"Maybe they'll be able to give us an address."

Claire wiped her eyes and retrieved her handbag from beside the sofa. She withdrew a small red book and flicked through the pages. Sara noted down the parents' address and phone number in Carla's notebook.

Carla returned carrying three mugs in her hands. She handed them around and retook her seat on the other side of the room.

"What about friends? Did William have a best friend?" Sara asked.

Claire shook her head. "No, not really. We had married friends who we visited together. He wasn't the type to go to the pub with his mates. Oh God, do you think he's responsible for killing all of them?"

"We really don't know that yet. All we know at this point is that he was seen leaving Janice and Lucas's home a few seconds before the fire started. There's more."

Claire turned to face her in the chair. "What? Please tell me, I need to know."

"Janice and Lucas were murdered."

"No!" Claire screamed. Her hand raised to her face and then instantly dropped to her lap a few times, as if she was unsure what to do with it. "Why? They were the sweetest couple. My God, what about Troy?"

"He died in the fire also." Sara decided not to tell her about the wounds he'd incurred prior to his death.

"They all died together," she whispered as the truth sank in.

"Yes. Is there anything else you think we should know about William that could possibly lead us to his whereabouts?"

"No, nothing. He tried to tell me where he was staying, but I didn't want to know. The court must have thought his behaviour was odd, too, because they issued a restraining order against him. Maybe his parents will be able to help."

"Does he have any other relatives living in the area?"

"No, no one." She shook her head adamantly.

"Is there anywhere else you can stay temporarily until we can track him down?"

"What? You think he's going to come after me?"

Sara shrugged. "To be on the safe side, I'd rather move you and your daughter from here, just for a few days."

"I could stay with my mum, but I'd rather not put her in danger."

"I can understand that. Let me see what I can do for you. I'll make a call now." Sara left the room and went into the kitchen of the house so her conversation couldn't be overheard. She rang the station and asked to speak to DCI Price. Her secretary put the call through. Sara apprised the chief of the nature and outcome of her visit and asked, "I need to put this woman in protective custody, ma'am. A possible safe house. Do we have one available?"

"I agree. It seems likely her ex will come after her soon. Let me make a few calls for you and ring you back."

"I was hoping you'd say that. Thank you, ma'am." She ended the call and returned to the lounge. "I'm waiting on a call back, Claire. I don't suppose you have a photo of William lying around, do you?"

Claire thought for a moment and then raised a finger. "I have somewhere. I took all the photos down when he left the house. I didn't want Gareth feeling awkward. There's one sitting beside Amelia's bed." She raced out of the room and up the stairs. The floor creaked overhead, and then she came back down carrying a framed photo of their prime suspect.

"Can we keep this?"

"Yes, of course. I hope it helps. Should I pack a bag for us, me and Amelia?"

"I think you should."

When Claire left the room, Sara lowered her voice and said, "Can you call the station? Get one of the team searching for Gareth Watson."

Carla fished out her phone and rang the station. Sara heard her asking a colleague to put an alert out for Gareth as if from a distance, her thoughts lingering with the poor families at the centre of their enquiries who had lost their lives. How could William kill the people closest to him? Why? In some cases, he'd actually tortured them as well, the heartless bastard. Again, why?

Carla hung up. "They're going to do a thorough search." Within seconds, Carla's phone rang.

They glanced at each other expectantly.

"Put it on speaker but turn it down," Sara instructed.

She got closer to Carla, and they bent their heads to listen as Carla accepted the call.

"Hi, Marissa, what have you found out?"

"I have a Gareth Watson showing up as being admitted to hospital yesterday evening. He arrived at A&E with a knife wound."

"Damn. Why didn't they ring us?" It was a rhetorical question from Sara. "Okay, what ward is he on now, Marissa?"

"The men's ward, boss."

"Right, once we're finished here, we'll shoot over there. We're trying to sort out a safe house for Claire and her daughter to stay at until we find William. Get the team to pull out all the stops to find him. He's violent according to his wife; however, I think we're all well aware of how violent and dangerous he can be."

"I'll let the others know, boss," Marissa replied.

Carla pressed the End Call button and let out a long sigh. "Do we tell her?"

"We're going to have to. She'll want to visit him." Sara's mind whirred. If they took Claire to hospital before depositing her at the safe house, she could call in to see how her father was at the same time. A little unprofessional, but it would seem daft not to as she was in the vicinity.

"What are you thinking?" Carla interrupted her thoughts.

"We'll take her to see Gareth. You can stay with them while I visit my dad. That way I can go straight home tonight and not feel guilty about missing a visit. I'm knackered already. God knows what state I'm going to be in at six."

"Makes sense to me."

With the plan etched in place, all they had to do now was wait for Claire to pack her bag. Sara paced the lounge until the woman reappeared carrying two overnight bags.

"I think I have everything. I should go to the school, pick up Amelia."

"We can do that later, she's safe there. I presume they're aware that there is a restraining order in place?"

"They are. They've assured me that if William turns up, they'll call the police."

"Good. We have some news for you, Claire. Take a seat."

She collapsed onto the sofa and stared up at Sara. "What is it? What's he done now? Oh God, he hasn't hurt my mum, has he?"

"No. It's Gareth. The reason his phone was going into voicemail was because he's in hospital."

"What? Why?" Her hand covered her eyes. "No, don't tell me, I can guess. William. What's he done to him?"

"We're unaware of what type of injuries Gareth has; all we know is that he was stabbed and ended up in A&E last night. We'll take you there now, if that's what you want?"

"Yes, it is. Oh God, this can't be happening, not to me, to us. I didn't realise how dangerous he was. Yes, he slapped me around more times than I care to remember, but bloody hell, I had no idea he was capable of really hurting people. Did I do this? Have I sent him over the edge?"

"No, you mustn't think like that, Claire. It's not going to help matters. If you're ready, we'll set off now."

They were just getting in the car when Claire's mobile rang. "Hi, Mum, are you okay?"

Claire's gaze met Sara's. She motioned with her hand and mouthed to remain calm and to put the phone on speaker.

"I think so, dear. William is here. He wants to see you and Amelia."

Sara's eyes closed momentarily and then sprang open when Claire let out a scream. She rushed to the woman's side, fearful that her legs would give way underneath her as William's voice filled the air.

"If you want to see your mother again, Claire, you'll bring Amelia to me."

"William, please...please don't hurt my mother."

"I won't. As long as you do as I tell you. Pack a suitcase for you and Amelia. Then pick her up from school and meet me at the place where we had our first date. Can you remember where that was, Claire?"

"I...I think so. What time should we be there?"

"At three o'clock on the dot. A moment too late and...well, do I really have to fill you in on the details?"

"I love you, Claire," her mother shouted in the background.

"Don't hurt her, William. I'm begging you."

Sara extracted the phone from Claire's trembling hand and ended the call. Claire fell into Sara's outstretched arms.

"We've got this covered, Claire. We'll be with you every step of the way. There was no indication that he knows we're in contact with you."

Claire pulled out of Sara's arms. "Is that a good thing or a bad thing? I don't know. He's obviously deluded, out of his mind for what he's done to my friends. Oh God, now he has my mother."

"Please, you need to think positively. Thinking negatively will only make things seem a thousand times worse. We've got time to figure something out. Do you want to go to the hospital as planned, to see Gareth? I think we should. Maybe he can tell us something about William that we're missing."

"Yes, if you think that will help. Oh crap! My poor mother. If he hurts her..."

Sara nodded. "Don't think about that. Let's go."

CHAPTER 14

SARA COULDN'T HELP but feel emotional when she saw Claire race towards the bed and gently gather Gareth in her arms.

"It's okay. I'm all right, love. The doctors have seen to that. I'm sorry I didn't ring you. I should have, but my main priority was to get myself to hospital. They gave me pain medication that knocked me out all night. I only came around half an hour ago."

"Hush, there's no need for you to apologise. It was William who did this to you."

Gareth nodded and looked past Claire at Sara and Carla. "I know. He introduced himself before he stabbed me. Forgive me, I had to tell him that I wanted to end things with you. I only said it because I thought it would save my life. It's not true, I love you, Claire, even with that madman on the loose. Who's this?"

Sara flashed her ID. "Detective Inspector Sara Ramsey and Detective Sergeant Carla Jameson, Mr Watson. We're investigating several cases of arson that we believe were carried out by William Mawdesley. Can you tell us what he said to you?"

"I was just leaving work." He flinched as he struggled to get comfortable in the bed. "His car was parked across the back of mine, blocking my way. I approached him, ready to have a go, and he stepped out of his vehicle wearing a balaclava. I didn't have a clue who this person was, not until he ordered me to get back in the car. Then he started asking me about Claire. I twigged who it was then. He had a huge knife. I felt compelled to tell him what he wanted to hear."

"When did he stab you?"

"Not long after I admitted I told Claire I loved her within two weeks of knowing her." He clutched Claire's hand to his heart and winced. "It's true. I could never give you up, Claire. Please forgive me?"

"Nonsense, there's nothing to forgive, you did what you had to do. He left you to die after he'd stabbed you?" Claire asked, saving Sara the job of voicing the same question.

"Yes, if that car hadn't tooted its horn behind us...well, I don't think I would still be here today. As soon as his car left, I started the engine. I wanted to get out of there quickly in case he went around the block and came back to finish me off. I drove here right away. They rushed me in and took care of me immediately. I should have rung you, but there just wasn't the time. Everything happened in a blur. I lost a lot of blood on the way here. I'm so sorry."

Claire placed a hand on his cheek. "Stop apologising. We're together now. What's going to happen to you? Did he hit any major organs?"

"No, he missed my kidney by inches. They rushed me down to surgery. I forgot that part, sorry, my head is still foggy. They've stitched me up. I feel okay, except when I move. Thank goodness you found me. I would have got around to ringing you eventually."

"We're back together again now. Things are getting out of control." Claire glanced over her shoulder at Sara. "Can I tell him?"

"Yes. We'll leave you to it." Sara and Carla stepped away from the couple to give them a moment's privacy. "Ring the station. I want an officer guarding this ward, just in case William shows up here."

"On it now. Do you want to nip and see your father? We still have time, it's only ten o'clock."

"I'll be back in five minutes, I promise. ICU is one floor up."

"Take your time. As long as we can organise things from here, there shouldn't be any comeback if anyone else finds out. That's not likely to happen anyway."

Sara patted Carla's forearm. "Thanks, love. I appreciate it. I'll be back in a jiffy."

She left Carla placing the call to the station and rushed through the hospital's corridors to ICU. She sanitised her hands with the gel and entered the ward. The sister glanced her way and joined her at her father's bedside. His skin was grey and his cheeks puffy.

"Oh God, he looks awful."

"He's not, I promise he's doing well. His body is dealing with the pain, that's all. I wasn't expecting to see you until this evening."

"I was here visiting a victim of an assault and thought I'd pop in for a few minutes. If there's no change, then that's a good thing, right?"

"It is. It's still early days, Sara."

"Just you and I talking now. What's your take on his condition? I have broad shoulders, I can stand the truth."

The sister smiled. "I can see you're just like me. I think it's sixty/forty in your father's favour now."

She exhaled a relieved sigh. "Thank you, that's all I needed to hear. Maybe I'll be able to keep my mind fully on my job now. It's been so difficult for me, for all of us."

"You said that was to be between you and me. I'm trusting you not to say anything to the other members of your family, just in case complications rear their head and his health declines."

"I won't say a word."

The sister nodded and walked away.

Sara ran a hand gently down her father's cheek and whispered in his ear, "Come back to us, Dad. We all miss you. It's not time for you to leave us yet, old man." Kissing his pale cheek lightly, she turned and waved at the nurses sitting at their station and left the ward.

There was an enthusiastic spring in her step as she made her way back to the men's ward. Maybe her father would wake up soon and be transferred to the ward she was about to enter. Carla was standing close to the door, giving Claire and Gareth space to chat.

"That was quick, I wasn't expecting you back so soon."

"I had a word with the sister, and she shared some positive news, although I've been sworn to secrecy."

"Secrecy? As in you're not supposed to tell the other members of your family? Seems a bit off to me."

"Yeah, I asked her to be honest with me, expecting her to say he wouldn't be with us long. But she's given him a sixty/forty chance. That's good enough for me. It's a load off my mind anyway."

Carla smiled. "I'm so pleased for you. I know what a burden this has been on your shoulders."

Sara nodded at Claire and Gareth. "We should break this up soon. Time is running out, and there's a lot to organise before three o'clock comes around."

"I thought the same. What are we going to do with Claire?"

Still eyeing the couple, Sara replied, "She's going to have to stay with us at the station for the next few hours."

"Where?"

"In an interview room or an office that isn't in use. There's no way we can allow her near the incident room, not with things escalating at this rate. Who knows what her ex is going to do next? I'd rather she learned about what he was up to secondhand, not be in the thick of it."

"Good idea. It's a shame she can't stay here with Gareth. I think they'd both appreciate that."

"Not practical. She'll be fine. It'll be an inconvenience for a few hours that I'm betting she won't mind as long as she's safe and out of the clutches of that madman. I hope to Christ he doesn't hurt her mother. I need to ask her how they got on. Most men detest their mother-in-laws, don't they?"

Carla winced. "I never thought of that. It doesn't bode well."

"Right, I'll have a word with them, and we'll shoot off." Sara marched towards the bed. "Sorry to interrupt. We should be going now, Claire. There's a lot to arrange before the deadline, things I need to do back at the station and not over the phone." The last part wasn't true, but Claire wouldn't know that.

The couple shared a kiss and a gentle hug, and then Claire joined

Sara and Carla at the exit to the ward. They raced through the hospital and out to the car.

Carla opened the back door for Claire. "You might want to put your seat belt on. The boss is an erratic driver."

Sara laughed. "That's so not true, Claire."

The light-hearted banter put a momentary smile on Claire's face.

However, the journey was filled with a bubbling tension and very little conversation. When they arrived at the station, Sara had a quiet word with the desk sergeant and left Claire in his hands.

The second Sara and Carla walked into the incident room, Sara could tell things had become serious. The team had their heads down at their computers.

"Any news?" Sara asked.

Carla crossed the room to the vending machine and returned carrying two cups of coffee.

"Boy, I'm in need of this. Go on, hit me with it, team. Anything on Mawdesley's car yet? Or is that wishful thinking on my part?"

"I got a hit on an ANPR camera which highlighted his car in the centre of town. I lost it again as it went over the bridge. I'm trying my hardest to locate it now," Barry announced.

"Stick with it, Barry. We need that. I've got a few things I need to deal with in my office. Keep me informed with any updates." Sara took her coffee into the office and rang her contact at the ART unit.

He answered her call personally. "Hi, Sara, what do you need?"

"I've got a volatile situation on my hands. You've probably seen the case on the news. The recent fires?"

"Yeah, I caught something last night. How can I help?"

"The man who caused the fires also murdered some of the victims. We've been on his tail for a few days, but things just got out of hand. He's holding his ex-mother-in-law prisoner—no obvious jokes if you don't mind, I know how your mind works."

"I'll behave. Okay, that's bad. What's his agenda?"

"He wants his wife and child to join him at a location in the centre of town."

"Shit! What time are we talking here?"

"Three p.m. this afternoon. I know that doesn't give us much time to work something out."

"I'm all yours. Don't let that distract you. We've got you covered."

"Phew! I was more anxious about you guys not being free than anything else. Okay, I'm going to ask you to stand by for the next hour or so. Let me figure things out with my team and I'll get back to you. Thanks, Jack."

"No problem. Let me know what you need and when you need it."

Sara ended the call and decided to ring her mother quickly.

"Hello," Lesley answered the phone.

"Hi, it's me. Just a quick one to see how Mum is this morning?"

"She's up and about, although she's still a little stiff. Have you rung the hospital today? I was about to do that."

"I went one better. I had to take someone to visit a relative in hospital and popped down to ICU while I was there. No change, which I think we have to take as a positive."

"You think? I'm not so sure. The longer he's unconscious, the worse his condition is, isn't it?"

"I don't think so, love. Try not to look at it that way. He's in the best place, and they're monitoring him twenty-four hours a day. They'll ring us if there's any major difference either way." She was aware she was bullshitting her sister, but what else could she do?

"I suppose you're right. I'll wait until Tim gets here later and pop down to the hospital this evening."

"If you want to. I don't think there's any need for you to do that, though, love."

"I can't not visit him, Sara," Lesley bit back. "Sorry, I didn't mean to have a go. I feel so useless."

"You're not being useless. Mum's needs are greater than Dad's at present, that's all, Lesley."

"Okay. I'll let Tim know. Are you going to pop in on your way home?"

"Things are going to kick off here today. There's no telling what time I'll be leaving this evening."

"Okay. Don't worry about us. Tim and I will cover things at this end. Stay safe, Sara."

"Thanks. Give my love to Mum."

Carla entered the office as Sara was hanging up.

"Sorry, I didn't realise you were on the phone."

"I'm not. What's up?"

"An update on the suspect's car. Barry had a hunch when he couldn't spot the vehicle on any other cameras in the area and sent a patrol car out to have a scout around. They located it in Asda's car park."

"Okay, and?"

While the patrol car was on site, a man approached the officers to say that his car had been stolen while he was in the store shopping."

"That's more than a bloody coincidence."

"That's what we thought. Barry's checking the cameras now. We've got the reg number and the make and model. It's only a matter of time before we track it down."

"Excellent news. Damn, I need to ring the chief, bring her up to date on things. Thanks, Carla."

Sara had a change of mind and decided to visit the chief instead. She followed Carla out of her office and trotted along the corridor. Mary glanced up and smiled when she entered.

"Is she free?"

"She is. Go right in."

Sara knocked on the chief's door and stepped into the room when Price summoned her. "Hi, can I have a quick word?"

"Come in. I was about to ring you. I've had no luck finding accommodation for your young lady."

"No problem, ma'am. Things have taken another direction since I called you."

"Sit down. Tell me what's happened."

Sara sat and crossed one leg over the other. "Claire Mawdesley is downstairs at present in one of the interview rooms."

The chief frowned. "Why?"

"I didn't know what else to do with her. She received a call from her ex, the suspect. He's abducted Claire's mother and is requesting that Claire and their daughter Amelia meet up with him at three this afternoon."

"Bloody hell."

"Precisely. Not an ideal situation to be in. I've arranged for a response team to provide backup at the location. I have to firm up the details with Jack later. What I was coming to tell you is that we won't need a safe house for Claire now, at least I hope we won't. Who knows how this will turn out? I never thought it would end like this. By that I mean, we've only just figured out who the damn suspect is. He's jumped the gun on us, upped his game before we had a chance to close in on him."

"That's unfortunate. Now he has the upper hand, by all accounts."

"Hopefully not for long, ma'am. We've just found out that he's stolen another vehicle. Fortunately, we have the car details. My guys are trying to track it down now."

"Will you try and grab him before the deadline?"

"I think we should. He's arranged to meet Claire in a busy part of town. We know he's dangerous. Oh, I forgot to say, he's put Claire's boyfriend in hospital, too. He's fine. Mawdesley stabbed him a few times but thankfully missed any major organs."

"He sounds like a nutcase to me. I need you to be extra vigilant out there, promise me."

"I will. Don't worry about me. Right, I'd better get back to it."

"Keep me informed how things progress—when you can, of course."

Sara smiled and left the room. She stopped off at the ladies' toilet on her way. It was nearing one o'clock by this time. Her stomach rumbled a little, which made her wonder if Claire was hungry shut away downstairs in the interview room. She nipped back to the incident room, took the orders for sandwiches from her team and ran downstairs to check on Claire.

She'd been crying. Her eyes looked sore when she glanced up at Sara. "Any news?"

"Yes and no. He's swapped vehicles, trying to fool us, I suspect, but we're onto him. Are you hungry?"

"I am but I doubt I'll be able to keep anything down."

"You should try. What sandwich do you want?"

"Ham and tomato." She scrabbled for her purse in her bag.

Sara held her hand up. "This is on me. White or brown?"

"I'm not bothered. That's very kind of you, thank you."

"I'll be back soon." Sara left the station and returned ten minutes later laden down with sandwiches and iced buns. She stopped off to ask the desk sergeant to supply a coffee for Claire and gave him the sandwich she'd bought for her.

"Shame I missed out on your generosity," he quipped.

"Sorry. Money's tight as it is."

"I'll let you off this time, ma'am."

When she walked into the incident room, Barry waved to get her attention. She dumped the food on Carla's desk.

"Distribute these around, will you?" She wandered over to Barry's desk and leaned over his shoulder. "What's up?"

"This was the final time I spotted the suspect's car. It's on the edge of town just going out into the countryside."

"Shit! Which basically means we've lost him, right?"

"In a word, yes. I can get a few patrol cars out there, see if they can find him."

"Do that. Blast, I was hoping to grab the bastard before the child gets involved. Best laid plans and all that."

"Leave it with me, boss."

She patted Barry on the back. "Take five minutes to eat your lunch, guys." Disappointed, she took her sandwich and cake into her office and perched on her desk, glancing out at the view as she ate. Only she struggled to swallow her food and gave up after attempting a few bites. "Bugger, where the heck can he be?"

"That's the first sign of madness." Carla chuckled.

She almost jumped out of her skin. "Cause me a heart attack, why don't you? Shit! Not the best choice of words in the circumstances."

"Sorry. You must be worried about your father."

"I am, but that's not what I was thinking about. Where could he be hiding, Carla?"

Her partner fell into the chair behind her.

Sara moved off the desk and sat in her seat. "He's obviously been living somewhere. We're going to have trouble locating where that is when he hasn't altered his address. I checked with DVLA just in case. He hasn't changed his address on his licence either."

"Naughty boy. That's a thousand pound fine heading his way."

Carla sniggered. "That'll be the least of his worries when we catch up with him. How's it going to go down?"

"The meeting? No idea. I need to figure that out with Jack, he's the response expert. I'll have to pass the baton over to him at the scene."

"What if things go wrong and someone gets hurt?"

"We can't think that way, Carla. We need to remain upbeat about the outcome. Hopefully, once the suspect sees his wife and child, that will be the end of it."

"Ya think?"

Sara shrugged. "Maybe I'm trying to remain optimistic about all of this. Why would he hurt his wife and child?"

"His *ex-wife* and child," Carla reminded her.

Sara ran a hand over her face. "You hear so many horrendous stories about fathers killing their children when they can no longer see them. I'm hoping this doesn't turn out to be one of those occasions. He's twisted enough—look what he's done already to their family friends, people he knew well. Why? We still haven't figured out that part yet."

"I know, it hadn't gone unnoticed. Will the response team take him down if he attempts to harm the child?" Carla asked, concern showing in the slight creases in her features.

"Without a doubt. I'm on tenterhooks just thinking about it. There's no way I could finish that damn sandwich." She picked up what she perceived as being the offending item and threw it in the bin.

"Hey, that was a waste. You could have saved it for later."

167

Sara fished the sandwich out of the bin and slid it across the table towards her partner. "Feel free to dig in."

"Gross. No thanks, I'm fussy where my food comes from."

Sara laughed and tossed the sandwich in the bin for the second time in as many minutes. "There's no pleasing some folks."

CHAPTER 15

William looked at his watch for the umpteenth time. It was only ten past one, almost two hours left before the deadline. He paced the floor in front of his captive who was tied to a chair. Between her and the voices in his head, he felt like his mind was on the brink of exploding.

"Please, William, all this is so unnecessary. Untie me, the rope is cutting into my wrists. What could I do? Overpower you? That's not likely, is it?"

She's trying to trick you. Once you've untied her, she'll find something to bash you over the head with.

I agree, don't trust the bitch. She's a devious witch.

"Shut up! The lot of you, just shut the fuck up!"

Sharon glanced around her. He could tell she was confused but he couldn't enlighten her. He refused to do that as he tried to block out the confounded voices. They were persistent buggers. Jubilant when the danger increased. He shook his head and hoped against hope they wouldn't drive him to do something stupid at three o'clock when he met up with Claire and Amelia.

He walked over and removed the hammer from the table. He returned to stand in front of her, the hammer raised.

Do it!

Kill her. Get it over with!

"No, William. Please, don't do this. I'll do anything you ask of me."

He growled and dropped the hammer on the floor, confusion swamping his mind, blocking out the voices for a few seconds.

"William, talk to me. Why are you doing this?"

His gaze locked on to hers and narrowed. "You deserve what's coming to you, Sharon. You shouldn't have interfered in our marriage. I used to like you."

Sharon gasped. "I had to intervene. Your marriage had become a sham. Claire told me how violent you'd become since losing your job. It wasn't her fault. You had no right taking your foul mood out on her. All she's ever done was love you. You're the one who destroyed that love. The only thing I'm guilty of is making her see the truth."

"You don't understand what it's like to feel so unwanted, first by your employer and then your own wife. I used to like you, Sharon. Respected you even, right up until the day you stood in my house and ordered me out of it. In front of my precious daughter, too. How could you do that?"

Sharon bowed her head in shame. "I'm sorry. I realise now what a mistake that was. William, I was only protecting my daughter. It's what parents do; it's their role in this life. Surely you can understand that? I couldn't sit back and watch while you knocked Claire around. I had to protect her, protect both of them. A man who lays his hands on his wife…well, he isn't a man, not in my book. Claire's father would never have sunk to such levels."

"It was out of *desperation*. I didn't know what I was doing. My mind was all over the place. I regretted my actions after every time."

"Once, once I might have been able to forgive but at the end of your relationship it was becoming a regular occurrence. You couldn't expect Claire to put up with that. Why should she? She had to protect her child. Have you ever hurt Amelia?"

William fell silent.

Sharon sobbed.

"I didn't mean to. She pushed my buttons one day, and I lashed out."

"You're an animal! How could you do that to my granddaughter? How could you do it to an innocent child?"

"I regretted it as soon as I did it. You have to believe me."

"I don't. You should never have lashed out in the first place. Parents need to dig deep, control the temper that builds within. It's tough at times, but to hit a child…"

"Shut up! I feel bad enough as it is without you having your say. I love that child like nothing else on this earth. I cherish her. We all make mistakes throughout our lives. That was my biggest one. That and losing my job. I had no control over that, but the devastation it caused fractured my world."

"You're trying to justify your actions when you should never have been in the situation in the first place. We all have to deal with disappointment during our lives, but it's the way we respond that is the key to our success. To give in and not have the determination to make up for those disappointments shows you were never capable of loving my daughter the way she deserved to be loved."

William glared at Sharon, and before he knew what he was doing, he slapped her hard around the face, her head whipping to the side. "How dare you. I gave your daughter everything when we were together. It wasn't my fault I lost my job. Her love for me died that day. She refused to stick to her vows, the vows we recited together in church. She destroyed me by ordering me out of the house. And as for our friends…"

"What about your friends?" Sharon asked, slowly turning her head back to face him.

"They cut me off. Refused to take my calls. I had to…"

"To what, William? What did you do?"

"*They* made me do it. I didn't do anything, it wasn't me, it was the voices in my head driving me on."

"What did the voices make you do, William?"

"They made me end their lives. I didn't know what I was doing at the time. You have to believe me."

"Are the voices forcing you to hold me captive now, William?"

"Yes. You'd need to be inside my head to hear them. They make me do dreadful things. Drive me to kill for their satisfaction. I didn't want to kill any of them. Especially Troy, he didn't deserve to die like that. I wanted to take him with me, to care for him once Janice and Lucas were gone, but the voices turned on me, insisted that I should do things their way or else…"

"Or else what? What could the voices possibly do to you?" Sharon asked, fresh tears sliding down her flushed cheeks.

He paused to think over her suggestion. The voices had driven him to do so many horrendous things over the past week, he wondered at times if he would ever be capable of thinking for himself ever again in the future. He paced the floor, the voices breaking their unusual silence.

She's nailed you, mate. You blame us all the time, when the fault lies with you.

Yeah, you're incapable of thinking for yourself. All we do is guide you. It's harsh to blame us for your failings in this life.

You struck your child; we had nothing to do with that.

Yes, you! You did it!

He clawed at the stubble on his chin. "I didn't mean to hurt her. She laughed at me. I warned her not to, and she did it again."

"Who did? Amelia?" Sharon asked.

"Yes. I warned her and…she should have listened to me."

"She's a *child*, William. Children often push the boundaries. She's too young to recognise right from wrong in many scenarios. Children need our guidance, not be punished for their imperfections. What type of lesson is she going to learn from being struck by her father? No wonder she fears you now."

"I love my daughter. I regret striking her and want the opportunity to make amends for my unwarranted actions. I need to be with her, both of them, Claire and Amelia. I'm lost without them."

"And you believe this is the right way to go about that? By abducting and hurting me? You'll never be with them again, not in that sense. You've cooked your goose, William. The more you hurt me, the more distance you will put between you and them."

"Shut up! If you don't keep quiet, I'll have no other option than to kill you."

"Then you'll be guilty of not listening to a word I've said. My advice will be worthless. You should listen to me. I know how my daughter thinks. Hurt me, and you'll drive an even bigger wedge between you."

He towered over her, his face flushed with anger as he struck her again. "You don't know your daughter as well as I do. You know nothing, Sharon. Nothing!"

CHAPTER 16

IT WAS two-fifteen when Sara rallied the team around and went over the plan one final time. "Is everyone clear on what they have to do?"

The team either nodded or raised their thumbs.

"Okay, let's go. The ART will meet us at the scene. I don't have to tell you how important it is that we keep our distance on this one, do I? The response team will do their bit; we'll be there as backup only, to mop up after they've dealt with the suspect."

"That sounds bloody ominous," Carla replied, slipping on her jacket.

Sara shrugged. "We're going to pick up Claire's car en route to the school. We'll follow her to the rendezvous at a safe distance." She held her clenched fist in the air. "Let's do this."

All but Jill left the incident room. The team filed past Sara and left the building. Sara instructed Carla to wait in her car while she collected Claire.

She pushed open the door to the interview room. Claire was sitting in the chair, staring at the wall. She glanced Sara's way and smiled.

"Are you ready?"

Claire nodded and rose from her chair. "As I'll ever be. My nerves are jangling. All I keep thinking about is whether he's hurt Mum or not."

"It's best not to think about that. I know I sound like a broken record, but please, try and remain calm. He's probably going to test your resolve when you finally meet up with him. Hopefully, seeing you and Amelia will make him rethink his actions. If not, there will be enough of us there to ensure he doesn't do anything that we're not bargaining on."

"I hope you're right. I can't help thinking that Amelia and I are walking into a trap."

"He's the one doing that, believe me." Sara was desperately trying to keep the news about the ART being involved from her, fearing that sort of information would only make Claire's nerves worse.

Claire blew out a long breath. "I'm ready to go."

Sara stepped aside to let Claire pass and then touched her arm. Claire faced her.

Sara hugged her. "I think you need this. Be strong, Claire. We won't let him hurt you, either of you."

Claire pulled away from her. "Thank you. I haven't known you long but I trust you."

"Good."

They walked out of the station side by side, their heads held high and their shoulders back. They joined Carla in the car and drove Claire back to her house to pick up her vehicle. Then they followed her on the short journey to the school. Claire ran through the school gates and emerged a few minutes later carrying her daughter who was holding her school bag and a teddy in her arms. Mother and daughter were both smiling at each other.

Sara prayed they'd still be smiling once they met with William.

Claire strapped her daughter into the back seat of her Golf and set off towards the rendezvous point. Sara kept her distance, aware of Claire constantly keeping her in her sights through the rear-view mirror.

It wasn't long before Claire stopped her vehicle by the bridge and parked in the pay and display car park. Sara entered and parked at the farthest end, around fifty feet from Claire.

"Here we go. There are plenty of buildings around. Can you spot any of the response team?"

"I saw a couple on the roof as we drove in."

"I'll give Jack a call. See if he's got eyes on the suspect yet." Sara placed the call. "Jack, it's Sara Ramsey. How's it going?"

"We're in position. The suspect isn't here yet. Where are you?"

"In the car park. Claire and her daughter are here. They're just leaving the car now and making their way over to the bridge."

"Okay, it's going to be a waiting game until he shows up. It's five minutes to three, he should be here soon. I'll be in touch...wait, no, a car has just arrived. A red Ford Focus. That's the car he stole, right?"

"Sounds like it. We'll follow Claire at a safe distance."

"Leave it to us, Sara. Keep well back."

"I will. I promise." She ended the call and breathed out a sigh. "He's here."

Carla opened the door. "My heart is racing."

"So is mine. We'll hang back until Claire has turned the corner."

Sara exited the car and scanned the area, searching for the rest of her team. A few flashed lights highlighted their positions. Sara gave them the thumbs-up, and she and Carla rushed after Claire.

The large stone walls of the building ahead would give them the cover they needed.

Sara pressed herself against the wall. "This is good enough for now."

"For you maybe. I can't see a bloody thing," Carla replied, frustrated.

"Stop being such a crybaby. Shit, he's there, so is Claire's mother. He has a knife to her throat."

"Damn. That's not good, considering what he's done with a knife in the past."

"Ssh...let me listen."

"Yes, boss," Carla grumbled behind her.

It was only now that Sara noticed the sound of the traffic in the distance. It was drowning out the conversation Claire was trying to hold with William. "Shit! I can't hear what's being said. I need to get closer." She put her phone on vibrate and ran across the concrete path to a lower wall on the other side. Carla was hot on her heels. "Damn, this is crap. I need a better position." Keeping low, she darted behind a thick tree trunk.

Carla remained where she was.

"Who was that?" William shouted.

Sara peered around the tree. He was staring straight at her.

"Come out. Get out here, bitch."

Sara rolled her eyes at Carla and mouthed for her to stay back. She left her hiding place and raised her hands. "Okay, all is good, William."

The blade tore at Sharon's throat. Droplets of blood ran down her neck. "I told you to come alone, Claire. Why did you disobey me?"

"I'm worried, William. Please, don't hurt her. Let Mum go. I'll take her place."

"Mummy, Mummy, I'm scared. What's Daddy doing to Grandma?"

His daughter's voice seemed to have a profound effect on him. Tears ran down his face, and a smile appeared. "Hey, baby. I've missed you so much. Have you missed Daddy?"

Amelia ran behind her mother's legs, and she peered around them.

"William. Come on, give yourself up. Let's talk about this like adults," Sara shouted. Her phone vibrated in her pocket. She knew who the caller would be—Jack, probably wanting to give her a bollocking.

"I'm tired of talking. Sharon will tell you that, won't you, Sharon?"

"Please, don't hurt me any more, William."

Sharon's voice cracked under the strain.

"Come on, William. No one wants to hurt you. There are ways of dealing with this issue. Put the knife down and let Sharon go."

"No, I won't do it. Who are you?"

"I'm someone who can give you a safe passage out of here, if that's what you want. But you're going to have to release Sharon in order for that to happen."

"You haven't answered my question: who are you? No, wait, I recognise you. You're the copper in charge, right?"

"Yes. I'm the senior investigating officer involved in your case. No one else needs to get hurt, William. Give yourself up, for your daughter's sake. Think about what this is doing to her. You're baffling her. She doesn't understand why you're trying to hurt her grandmother. Drop the knife, and we'll sit down and chat."

His head tilted, then he shook it and muttered something she couldn't hear.

"The voices, they're the ones who tell me what to do, not you."

Fuck! He hears voices. How the hell am I supposed to combat them?

"Did the voices tell you to kill your friends, William?"

"Yes. All of them. I didn't want to do it. They were guilty, though."

"Guilty of what, William?"

He paused for a moment or two and then said, "Turning their backs on me when I needed them the most. Janice and Lucas even rescinded their invitation to their engagement party. That hurt more than anything else. Why would they do that to me?"

"I don't know. Perhaps the party became too costly for them and they had to make a few cuts."

"Yes, that was it, William," Claire piped up. "Costs were spiralling out of control. Janice told me she'd had to cut back on the invitations. You weren't the only one. Three of my friends also had their invites rescinded."

This information appeared to rock William. His glance darted between Sara, Claire and Amelia. "It's not true, you're just saying that."

"I'm not. I swear it's the truth, William," Claire replied, her voice calm as she clung to her child.

"See, it was a simple mistake, William. Don't let there be any others. Let Sharon go, and we'll talk about what's happened. Deal with the consequences together," Sara shouted.

"I'll let Sharon go, but first Claire and Amelia need to come to me. I want to hold my daughter. The authorities have prevented me from doing that. I miss holding her in my arms. The smell of her at night when I tuck her in bed after she's had her bath."

"We can arrange that, William. First, you need to let Sharon go."

"No. She's my security. Without her, I have no bargaining power. Claire, bring Amelia here."

Claire glanced over her shoulder at Sara.

"You don't need her permission. Come here," William snapped.

Sara's pulse rate rose. *Crap, if she steps forward, there's no way the ART can take the shot. There will be too many bodies in the way.* Her phone vibrated again; she couldn't answer it, not now. She was on her own. Sara took a few steps forward while William's gaze was locked on Claire.

He spotted the movement and again nicked Sharon's throat with the knife. "No funny business—you stay where you are, cop. Don't make me add to the body count."

"I won't, I promise. Look, William, this situation isn't doing anyone any good. Let Sharon go. Let's sit around a table and talk about this rationally. I'll have a word with the authorities, tell them the lengths you're prepared to go to just to see your daughter, to have her in your life. They'll listen to me, I'm sure they will. Come on, William, work with me here."

He hesitated and remained quiet for what seemed like ten minutes or so, but in reality, it was only a few seconds. In that time, Sara's brow broke out in sweat, and her palms became clammy.

"I'll let Sharon go if Amelia comes to me and gives me a cuddle."

Claire peered over her shoulder at Sara, her eyes wide in objection.

Sara smiled reassuringly at Claire and briefly shook her head, hoping that William didn't notice the action. Her gaze drifted back to William, and in her peripheral vision she spotted an armed officer approaching him, knees bent, gun pointed at William's head.

Shit! Let her go, William, for your own good, let her bloody go.

"William, you know full well we can't let Amelia come to you, not when you're holding a weapon. Drop the knife, and we'll have no option but to reconsider."

"Don't let her near him," Sharon shouted. All of a sudden, she bravely pulled away from William, believing he was distracted, no doubt. She was at arm's length. He slashed her cheek with the knife.

A red dot appeared on his chest, and Sara knew it was all over when two shots rang out, one from the officer sneaking up on him from behind and another from what appeared to be the roof of a building off to her left.

The next few moments were frantic. Claire and Amelia both screamed. Footsteps pounded behind her—it was Carla.

"Quick, get them out of here, back to the car. I'll see what I can do for him."

Sara sprinted to make sure Sharon was all right. She was. "Stay there, I need to check William."

The armed officer was standing over him, his gun pointing at his chest. "All right, stand back, let me try and help him."

"It's you who should stand back, ma'am," the officer shouted.

Sara shook her head, and her phone vibrated. She ignored it. Instead, she got down on her knees and rested William's head in her lap. "William, stay with us."

"I'm going. There's no hope for me," he whispered.

Her need to understand his motive was prominent in her mind. "Tell me why? Why did you kill them, William? What possessed you to kill your friends?"

"The voices. They drove me to do it. They told me they were all laughing at me. Mocking me for what I'd lost. I was scared of being alone. Everyone cut me off. I couldn't see my daughter; Claire took out a restraining order. I needed to see Amelia, and all of our friends were laughing at me. I was left with nothing." As he spoke, his breathing became ragged.

Sara swept a hand over his damp brow, feeling sorry for the man who had once had everything and lost it all. She detested what he'd been forced to do, but a part of her could understand the despair that had driven him. Before she could ask anything else, he took his final breath and slipped away.

She glanced up at the armed officer. "Lower your weapon, he's gone."

The officer shook his head and maintained his position. Sara gently eased William's head off her lap and placed it on the ground, then she went to help Sharon to her feet.

Jack appeared on the scene and instructed his man to stand down. "Are you all right?" he called over to Sara and Sharon.

"She will be. I'll call an ambulance."

He nodded. There was nothing else to say about the incident, which Sara hoped would have ended differently, given what William had revealed. Maybe she was wrong about that, who knew?

The ambulance arrived, and Claire and Amelia followed it back to the hospital where Sharon's wounds would be seen to.

Sara and Carla drove back to the station. The team were all subdued when they arrived as Carla had relayed the news prior to their arrival. No serving police officer ever felt good when a suspect died at a scene, no matter what heinous crimes they had committed.

"Let's wrap the case up, folks. Spend the rest of the day filling out the laborious paperwork. I'll be in my office, writing up my own report. A coffee wouldn't go amiss, partner."

Carla nodded.

Sara entered her office and perched on the edge of her desk, glancing out at the grey sky and noting the speed of the dark clouds overhead. Carla tapped on the door and entered the room, placing her coffee on the desk behind her.

"It amazes me the lengths people will go to sometimes, although in William's case, I don't think he had a lot of choice in the matter."

"What? You're making an exception for him, in spite of him torturing and murdering his friends like that? Are you mad?"

Sara turned to face her partner and raised her eyebrow. "Possibly. None of us can honestly say we wouldn't have reacted the same way in the same position, dealing with voices intent on causing harm to people we love and cherish the most." She pointed to her temple. "Who knows what really goes on up here for some people who have been cast aside by society?"

Carla shrugged. "I suppose. Even so, those people didn't deserve to die."

"There's no doubting that."

EPILOGUE

IT HAD BEEN AN EMOTIONALLY DRAINING day for Sara. She was adding the finishing touches to her report when her mobile rang. She glanced at the caller ID to find it was Lesley.

"Hey, you. I'm just packing up. I was going to drop in and see Mum on the way home. Can I pick up anything from the supermarket for you on the way?"

"Sara. We're at the hospital. Can you get here right away?"

Her chair scraped. She wrestled into her jacket and was halfway across the incident room before she answered, "What's wrong? Is it Dad? Stupid question, I'm on my way." She turned to her team and shook her head. "I've got to go. I'm needed at the hospital. Good work today, team. See you in the morning."

"Do you need me to drive you?" Carla asked.

"No. I'll be fine." She raced down the stairs and en route she rang Mark. "Hi, just a quickie. I've been summoned to the hospital. I know I'm asking a lot but can you join me? I have a feeling I'm going to need your support."

"Crap! Setting off now. I'll see you soon."

She hung up, grateful that Mark was willing to drop everything when she needed him. *Please, please, don't let Dad die. I couldn't cope with losing him, not now, on top of everything else I've had to deal with over the past few years.*

Thankfully, the traffic was working with her for a change and was lighter than she'd anticipated at this time of night. She arrived at the car park, stopped at the barrier to retrieve a ticket and locked the car. She was surprised to see Mark standing at the entrance waiting for her. "How the hell did you get here so fast?"

"I was in town collecting some supplies for the surgery. Sorry, I should have told you. Let's get in there and see how he is."

They held hands, tore through the entrance and were standing outside ICU applying the antibacterial gel within minutes. Sara peered through the portal window and gasped. The curtain had been drawn around her father's bed. She'd tried to brace herself for bad news on the journey over there, but nothing could have prepared her for this. Her heart was pounding so hard she thought she was about to suffer a heart attack of her own.

Mark pushed the door open and slung a comforting arm around her shoulder. He pulled back the curtain. What he revealed took her breath away. She turned to face him. He smiled and nodded.

"You knew?" She punched him in the stomach and then rushed forward to smother her dad in kisses. "Oh God, I thought we'd lost you."

"Obviously wasn't my time to go yet, darling."

She cuddled her mother who looked less frail now her father was back with them. "I'd built myself up for bad news. I'm so pleased I was wrong. How are you, Mum?"

"I'm fine. Getting stronger every day. I'll be back to normal now your father is going to be okay."

"Hopefully I will be after the surgery," her father replied.

The curtain was drawn back by a nurse. She was accompanied by a porter. "What surgery?" Sara asked.

"Your father is going down for a triple bypass," the nurse replied.

"What? Now?"

Her mother clutched her arm. "We knew this day would come

eventually, Sara. Let's get it out of the way and get your father back on the road to recovery soon, eh?"

"I suppose." She stepped aside and linked arms with Lesley.

"He'll be fine, sis, you'll see."

She pecked Lesley on the cheek. "Where's Tim?"

"At home."

"Drunk as usual?" she muttered so their parents couldn't hear.

"He's got issues. Don't be harsh on him."

Sara glanced at her and shook her head. "You're too soft on him. He needs a good talking to about where his responsibilities lie." She bit her tongue as William's face entered her mind. "Okay, forget I said that. We'll be there for him, if he needs help."

"Good. It's up to him to ask us for that help, sis."

"Agreed. I'll never come down heavy on him again, not after what happened at work today."

Lesley tilted her head. "What was that?"

"I'll tell you later."

The three women kissed her father, and Mark shook his hand, then the porter took him down for surgery.

The following four hours seemed an eternity to contend with. They finally received the news from the surgeon that her father was in the recovery room around nine-thirty that evening.

The surgery had been a complete success, but the surgeon warned that the recovery process would be a lengthy one, and that they would need to be patient with her father.

That didn't matter to Sara, at least her father was still alive.

They had to be grateful for small mercies. Her family was complete again.

THE END

NOTE TO THE READER

NOTE TO THE READER

Dear reader,

Wow, this was a tough case for Sara to solve amidst the personal problem thrown at her. It just goes to show, no one knows the true impact on another person's life when a marriage ends.

Sometimes it's a tough lesson to learn in this life.

Sara and her team will be back in the near future, for now, if you haven't already read it, why not read the first book in the award-winning, bestselling Justice series, CRUEL JUSTICE I'm sure you'll enjoy the ride.

As always, thank you for choosing to read my book out of the millions available today. If you could find it in your heart to leave a review, I'd truly appreciate it, I read every last one of them.

M. A. Comley

KEEP IN TOUCH WITH THE AUTHOR

Sign up to M A Comley's newsletter for announcements regarding new releases and special offers.

http://smarturl.it/8jtcvv

Or follow on:

Twitter

https://twitter.com/Melcom1

Blog

http://melcomley.blogspot.com

Facebook

http://smarturl.it/sps7jh

BookBub

www.bookbub.com/authors/m-a-comley

ABOUT THE AUTHOR

M A Comley is a New York Times and USA Today bestselling author of crime fiction. To date (May 2019) she has over 90 titles published.

Her books have reached the top of the charts on all platforms in ebook format, Top 20 on Amazon, Top 5 on iTunes, number 2 on Barnes and Noble and Top 5 on KOBO. She has sold over two and a half million copies worldwide.

In her spare time, she doesn't tend to get much, she enjoys spending time walking her dog in rural Herefordshire, UK.

Her love of reading and specifically the devious minds of killers is what led her to pen her first book in the genre she adores.

Look out for more books coming in the future in the cozy mystery genre.

Facebook.com/Mel-Comley-264745836884860
Twitter.com/Melcom1
Bookbub.com/authors/m-a-comley
https://melcomley.blogspot.com

Made in the USA
San Bernardino, CA
10 May 2019